"Can you still deny, sir, that this woman is your mother?"

Emily spoke softly as she drew James into the corridor.

"How else could she know all these things about your childhood?" she continued.

James grasped the ends of his waistcoat. "I admit that she makes a good case for herself but—"

His confused expression was so delightful that Emily found it hard to press a serious argument. She tucked a stray curl into place and regarded him with amusement.

"What of the whistle?" she said.

The earl was silent for a moment, then reached into his pocket and extracted a silver bird on a delicate chain.

"Is this what you mean?" he asked.

"How should I know?" she answered. "Is it a whistle?"

He held it to her mouth. "Blow."

Emily did as he instructed and was rewarded with a trill of musical notes. Before she could say anything, he took it from her and put it to his own lips and gently blew a few notes.

His eyes darkened with an intensity which shortened her breath. She knew he wasn't thinking of the birdsong. As clearly as if he had said so, Emily knew that the whistle was still warmed by the taste of her mouth.

Books by Phyllis Taylor Pianka

HARLEQUIN REGENCY ROMANCE

HARLEQUIN INTRIGUE

THE CALICO COUNTESS

PHYLLIS TAYLOR PIANKA

Harlequin Books

TORONTO • NEW YORK • LONDON
AMSTERDAM • PARIS • SYDNEY • HAMBURG
STOCKHOLM • ATHENS • TOKYO • MILAN

Once again,
to Ed.

Published September 1990

ISBN 0-373-31134-6

CHAPTER ONE

THE CITY TEEMED with the stench of decaying rubbish imprisoned under a cloud of smoke from coal fires left burning against the late-afternoon chill. Emily Merriweather Harding tucked her hands into the worn beaver muff and edged closer to the building. It was warmer here and less conspicuous. Had they found her? She had taken a circuitous path from Threadneedle Street on the chance that she was being followed, but even then she had come upon the same group of young toughs. Whether they had seen her she didn't know, for fortune prevailed and she ducked behind a fishmonger's wagon until the thugs had disappeared. And now the rain had begun to fall in tiny droplets which clung to the wisps of gold-brown hair curling around the brim of her bonnet.

As she passed an open doorway, the smell of boiled cabbage assaulted her senses, causing her empty stomach to lurch uncertainly. She hated cabbage, but the thought of it piled high on a plate with a trickle of butter running down the side made her mouth water. Butter. It was weeks since she had tasted butter—or milk—or meat, for that matter.

A man stumbled out of a building just ahead of her and stopped to stare. At first glance he appeared old, though his state of dishabille and ragged beard made it difficult to tell. As she drew closer she realized her first impression was wrong. His eyes, bleary and red though they were, gave evidence of the man's youth. He smelled strongly of Blue Ruin or Strip-me-naked. Scotched, he was, or so he pretended. Had he recognized her? She had been flammed before. This time she would take no chances.

Settling her chin deep within the folds of her cloak, she hurried across the street. The rain continued with an oily mist that slimed the cobblestones and filled her nostrils with a metallic stench. Now and then she glanced backwards, but there was no sign that she was being followed.

Her heart slowed to a normal pace. How long must she go on like this, in constant fear that Grimstead or his agents would find her? Fear of discovery made it almost impossible for her to look for work, and now the few shillings in her purse were scarcely enough to pay for three more weeks' rent on her attic room.

The devil take the man! How many lives had Grimstead ruined with his thieving ways? She wouldn't go back to work for him, nor would she pay the money he claimed she owed to him. But if he found her... She shuddered. There were other younger, prettier women who had fared less well than she. Some of them wasted away now in Newgate Prison.

A distant shouting drew her up short and she whirled round to investigate. The mob of jackanapes had found her and were rapidly approaching. She started to run, and then, finding an unlocked wrought-iron gate leading to a dark passageway, she stepped inside. Something was different this time. A woman's voice shrilled above the clatter of stones and the thunk of barrel staves.

Emily chanced a cautious look, then breathed a sigh of relief. It wasn't she they were chasing. An elderly woman, a ragamuffin in a calico dress, was weaving her way down the slippery street while at the same time trying to dodge the stones and filth which were being thrown by a group of young boys. The woman seemed close to the back side of the ladder as she tried to keep from being surrounded by the dozen or more thugs.

Emily felt a twinge of guilt over her own sense of relief at not being the victim. It was quickly replaced by a feeling of outrage that anyone should be treated so badly, especially an old woman. Pushing back her fear, Emily stepped out of the doorway and grabbed the woman by the arm. She whirled and would have struck her, but Emily shoved her through the gateway, then stepped between her and the mob.

"See here, that's quite enough! Are you such ninnies that you can only pick on cripples and old ladies? Be gone with you or I'll send the Charlies after you." Before they could recover from their surprise, Emily ducked inside the alleyway and slammed the gate after her. Once the iron bar was shoved home, there was no way the boys could follow.

Emily was trying to decide what to do next when the woman tapped her on the shoulder and spoke in a cool voice. "Young woman, how dare you refer to me as a cripple and an old lady? I demand an apology at once."

Emily was taken aback. She turned, surveying the woman with careful scrutiny. She *was* an old woman, but she was not crippled, as Emily had perceived. It soon became evident from the cloud of sherry which drifted up when the woman spoke, that she was well into her cups and had been for some time.

Emily smiled. "I do beg your pardon. I didn't mean to be rude. Are you all right?"

"All right? Of course I'm not all right. Any fool could see that I'm cold and hungry and have need of my hairdresser. And have you no manners, girl? You failed to curtsy before you spoke to me."

Emily choked back a laugh. She dropped a practised curtsy and was rewarded with a regal nod from the elderly urchin in the soiled calico gown. "Very well." She nodded towards the gate. "I suppose I must thank you for routing those young ruffians, but what do you propose to do now?"

"I—I really haven't decided," Emily said.

"Surely you don't mean us to stand here all night? Those boys have no intention of leaving."

As if to emphasize the point the leader of the mob began running a barrel stave across the gate. The sound echoed loudly in the passageway.

"I fear you are right. They will not leave as long as we remain here." Emily looked down the long, dark walkway to a lighted opening at the far end. "I think perhaps we can get away from them by following this passageway to the next street."

The woman held herself severely erect and motioned with a graceful flick of her hand. "Very well. Lead on. I shall follow."

Emily chewed her lip to keep from laughing. This old woman with her torn and faded calico dress, stringy grey hair hanging in wild disarray, black stockings sagging over boots which had long ago worn through to the lining—this woman wore the air of Quality as no duchess ever had.

Blessedly, the iron gate at the other end of the alley gave way under heavy pressure and exited onto a street not far from where Emily lived. She ushered the woman into the open and closed the gate behind them.

"We're safe here, I think," Emily said. "Can you find your way home?"

"Home?" The woman looked dazed. "Indeed. Do you think I'm a complete fool? Of course I can find my way. I've been doing it for..." She paused. "Is this Brighton or Exeter?"

Emily groaned. "It's London, of course."

"London! Indeed, then I am almost home." The woman leaned against the iron fence, resting first one foot and then the other. "I would be the first to admit that it has been an excruciating journey. Tell me, girl, what year is it?"

"It's 1814, of course. And I think perhaps you'd better come home with me until we find out more about you."

"Nonsense. I have no time to waste with chitchat."

"But you said you were cold and hungry. I happen to have a bit of cheese and bread in my small larder. And my attic room is quite warm at this time of day." Seeing the woman begin to weaken, Emily pressed her advantage. "And I know we both would like to rest awhile."

"Very well, since you are so insistent. But only to please you and only for a brief visit, mind you. Then I must take my departure."

It was no easy task getting the woman to the house in Meecham Street, then up the three flights of stairs to the attic room where Emily had lived for the past five days. The woman was terribly weak and undernourished. She ate ravenously of the bread and cheese, then looked down the end of her nose. "I suppose you have no sherry?"

Emily carefully covered the remaining bread with a cloth and placed it in a metal box. Her voice was dry. "Sherry? Regrettably, the Prince Regent consumed the last of it when he stopped in this morning to ask my advice about the new tariff."

"Indeed? I wish I had been here. I haven't seen Prinny since he was a mere boy."

Emily gasped. She was trying to think of a quelling response when she looked over her shoulder and saw that the woman had fallen asleep at the table, her fingers still clutching a morsel of cheese.

The poor soul. She looked as if she had been trodden upon by Napoleon's army. And yet there was a hard-to-define quality about her, a certain sense of pride, of breeding. What was she to do with the woman? Emily wondered. She couldn't afford to keep her. She couldn't even afford to feed herself, let alone another person, especially one who appeared to be so addle-witted as to need a keeper. And yet she couldn't turn her into the street with darkness just a few hours away. But there was only one narrow cot to sleep on. Emily was hard-pressed to know what to do.

She looked around the tiny room with its daub-and-wattle walls, the straw-filled mattress, the dresser with its cracked bowl and pitcher, the hooks which held her few garments.

Thank God that Henry had not lived to see her in such precarious straits. He had been a good provider before he was struck down with consumption. It had taken him a long time to die, time during which their hoarded savings had gone to pay for his care. Everything was gone. Everything except the title. She pressed her fingertips together. Possessing a title without the blunt to go with it was like trying to light the dark with a wickless candle. Prudence had taught her to conceal her breeding, for in the marketplace there was no love lost between the lower class and the highborn.

She turned back to the table. "And speaking of the highborn, what am I to do with you, my little ragamuffin lady?" Emily expected no response. The woman had scarcely stirred where she rested at the end of the table.

Later when Emily tried to help her towards the bed, the woman thrust her away, refusing her help in no uncertain terms. At last Emily lay down on the cot and slept between bouts of her guest's most unladylike snores.

IF EMILY HOPED that dawn would bring a clarity of mind and softness of demeanour to the calico woman, she was wrong. Before her guest awakened, Emily went downstairs to beg a discarded gown from the landlord's wife. Though faded and of a pedestrian style, it was clean, mended, and should be a vast improvement over the calico. But Emily hadn't counted on her guest's muttonheadedness.

"Young woman, surely you jest. You can't expect me to wear someone's cast-off clothing. I have my position to think of. The fact that I am presently without funds does not signify."

Emily was fast getting her back up. "Perhaps you'll think differently when you want something to eat. Or is it your intention to hang on to my sleeve until someone more gullible comes along?"

"My dear girl, it's plain to see you haven't a sixpence to scratch with. I have no intention of remaining here. I do suggest, however, that you choose your language with care and remember to whom you speak."

Emily was more curious than offended. "And just who are you, if I may be so bold?"

"Dear me. I thought you knew, of course. Why... I'm Lady Marguerite, Countess of Berrington. I'm on my way to our London estate to be with my son, James Carstairs, the Earl of Berrington."

"Of course. How could I not have known?" Emily had passed by the lovely sprawling mansion in May-fair. Picturing this flapdoodle as lady of the manor was indeed too much to swallow and she could scarcely keep from laughing. "Forgive me, your ladyship. I didn't realize that calico was all the rage. Would you like me to dust your tiara?"

"You've no need to act pin-witted. You shall see, my dear. And I shall forgive your missish pelter since you saw fit to offer me protection for the night. Now if you will be so good as to brew a pot of tea?"

Although the so-called countess continued to insist that she had no intention of accepting Emily's hospitality for another day, she made no move to take her departure. If truth be told, Emily had little taste for broaching the subject when she saw how close to collapse her guest appeared to be.

For two days the woman stuck to Emily's side like cockleburs on a hound's belly. By the third day Emily knew she must sconce the reckoning or they would both starve. It was then she decided to take the woman to the London estate of Lord Berrington, the earl whose mother she claimed to be. He had the reputation of being an intractable man. The one time Emily had seen him gave credence to the reputation, but perhaps he would, out of common decency, offer some aid to the woman, whoever she might be. The possibility that she was indeed the Countess of Berrington was too remote even to court one's imagination.

When Emily revealed her intention to escort the countess to the Berrington estate, the old woman was overjoyed. "You shall see, my dear Emily. I'll have you looking fine as a fivepence when I am settled back in my home."

She studied Emily carefully. "Hmm. You're not all that bad to look at. Of course my son is a high stickler and I sometimes deplore his prosiness, but he is a good man and he will see to it that you are well provided for."

Emily carefully schooled her countenance. Prosiness, indeed! She had heard that the earl, although a highly eligible bachelor, was considered stuffy in the extreme. It would be interesting, at the very least, to see his expression when he was presented with this bundle of sherry-soaked calico who professed to be his mother.

Emily mused. *Now, if I were a few years younger I could pose as his daughter and* really *singe his buttons.* She giggled. Of course the idea was ridiculous, but it would have served him right after the way he had embarrassed her all those years ago at Heatherwood Castle.

She studied her softly rounded curves beneath the blue velvet chemise she had been wearing for the past four days. She had grown up since he had last seen her. Even so, chance would have it that he might remember the incident. Foisting an impostor on him would be sweet vengeance.

Revenge or not, the earl seemed to be her only possible hope of finding a home for—Emily grinned—the countess. It was that, or end up with a permanent copesmate, for it was clear that the countess had no intention of leaving Emily's protection in the near future.

SECOND THOUGHTS and the two hours it took to arrive at the Berrington estate in Mayfair did not augur well for what at the time had seemed like an inspired plan. The house was even larger than Emily had remembered. Built of red brick softened to a warm patina by time and the elements, the mansion rose three stories above parklike grounds. Tall chimneys looked down on peaked, grey-tiled roofs.

There were tears in the countess's eyes. "It's nearly the same as I remember it," she said, her voice shaking. "They've changed the draperies in the salon. The blue velvet I chose was imported from France to match the Chinese wallpaper. The earl and I discovered it when we visited the Orient. I do hope James hasn't replaced it, too." She clutched Emily's arm. "Oh, my dear. I've just had the most quelling thought. Could my son have married during my absence? Am I now the Dowager Countess?"

Emily shot her a surprised look. "I don't think so. If the earl had married it would be common knowledge. I've seen nothing in the *Times* about a wedding in the family."

The countess drew a shuddering sigh. "That comes as a considerable relief. Not that I object to James taking a wife," she quickly assured Emily. "He must soon do so in order to continue the line. It is only that my return home will in itself be a considerable shock. Getting to know my grown son is more than enough to contend with without the added problem of a new daughter-in-law."

Emily felt a stirring in the pit of her stomach. The woman was beginning to make sense. Was it possible that she really was—? No. It simply wasn't possible that this woman was Lady Carstairs, Countess of Berrington. Emily pulled her cloak around her and thrust out her chin. She had promised the woman to see this through and she would, no matter how discomfited she was beginning to feel.

An iron fence surrounded the mansion, but they found the gate locked against casual intruders. A bell-pull used to summon the keeper had somehow caught on a bar just out of Emily's reach.

"I suppose we could try the servants' entrance," she said, half to herself, but in truth she would have preferred to forget the whole plan.

"Nonsense, Emily. Using the servants' door would be too, too scaly. Wait. I'll find the key." In a flash the countess had unearthed a heavy metal key from beneath a half-buried flagstone. Despite the shaking of palsied fingers protruding from worn black gloves, she inserted the key into the lock and opened the gate. She then replaced the key beneath the stone and attempted to brush the grime from her hands.

"Well, don't just stand there looking moon-brained. Use the door knocker and summon the butler," she said as she motioned Emily to climb the entrance steps.

Emily, feeling too incredulous to speak, did exactly as she was told.

The sound of the door knocker reverberated deep within the cavernous halls of the house, and before the echo had stopped, the black-coated butler was already opening the door. Without waiting for him to acknowledge their presence, the countess stepped back in surprise.

"Oh! But you're not Emmet. And who might you be?"

The stiffly disapproving majordomo closed the door to a mere crack as if to avoid contaminating the house with alcoholic fumes. "Beggars and tradespeople are received at the rear door, madam."

The countess shoved a shoddy boot into the scant opening, successfully blocking his efforts to dismiss them. "Just one moment. Tell me your name, my good man. I presume you are new at your trade or I would see to it that you were immediately discharged."

The butler was enough taken aback that he opened the door a generous ten inches, just far enough to give the countess good purchase so that she was able to gain entry.

"Well, speak up, man."

His face was set in a grim line. "My name is Fredricks, madam, and I have been in the earl's employ for nearly twelve years."

"Indeed! Then be good enough to summon him at once."

"I cannot do that, madam. Please be considerate enough to take your leave before I must summon the constable."

Emily's courage returned in the face of such snobbery. She put her hand on the countess's arm to stay her. "Fredricks, I don't think you quite understand the seriousness of the situation. The count—my friend here is not as strong as she appears. She is in need of a place to sit down. If his lordship is at home, I strongly beseech you to summon him before it's too late."

"Unfortunately my master is away. If you wish to see him, you may leave your card." He reached a white-gloved hand for a silver salver and stiffly presented it to them.

The countess pushed the salver aside with a less-than-immaculate gloved hand and sniffed. "I've ordered cards but they have yet to arrive. We'll wait." With that, she marched down the hall with the butler and two footmen trailing quickly behind her. The butler managed to reach her side and turn her in the general direction of a narrow corridor leading, Emily suspected, to the back stairs. Mustering all his dignity, he opened a door and ushered the countess inside.

Fredricks was looking a little wild-eyed by the time Emily reached the door. "If you will be so good, madam." He clicked his heels and bowed her inside. The countess was already enthroned in a stiff-looking straight-backed chair which seemed to go perfectly with her personage. She was completely undaunted by her cold reception.

"Some sherry, Fredricks. Then you may go, but see to it that James is made aware of my presence forthwith."

"Of that you can be assured, madam. May I tell him the nature of your business?"

"Just tell him his mother has come home."

It was as if she had said Princess Caroline was playing darts in her unmentionables in the middle of Grosvenor Square. An expression of such amusement crossed Fredricks's face that Emily was ready to take her departure. But then the butler closed the door with acceptable haste, given the circumstances, and the women were left alone.

The countess looked around her at the meagre furnishings and sniffed loudly. "From the looks of the chairs and carpet I collect he's stigmatized us as dirty dishes. I believe I recall that we used this room when we interviewed prospective servants.''

Emily settled down, resting her arms on the wobbly tabletop. ''What does it matter, Countess? We're here, aren't we? It's what you wanted, though heaven only knows what the earl will say when he sees you. Chances are we'll be lucky to escape with our skins intact.''

''Don't be a chucklehead. He's my son, after all. He wouldn't dare turn us out into the street. Take off your bonnet. It's hardly suitable for the season.''

Emily hesitated, knowing she was ill-advised to do as the countess bade, but the wool-lined velvet bonnet was heavy and the air in the small room was warm. She pulled it off and laid it on the table next to her reticule.

''There, much better,'' the countess said in a motherly tone. ''You have splendid hair, you know. It just needs a little nipping away at the ends. I'll have my hairdresser see to it after I'm settled in.''

Emily was exasperated. ''Stop that! You'll have me believing that you really are the Countess Berrington.''

''I beg your pardon!''

Emily sighed. ''If you were the countess, the butler would have recognized you.''

''He's new. Emmet was *my* majordomo.''

''New? He claims to have been twelve years in the Berrington family's employ.''

''Just so. Where is that sherry? Confound the man. I'll have him sacked for such incompetence.''

''Suffice it to say that he probably thought we were both already well into our cups. One of us certainly smells that way.'' Emily fanned the fumes. ''You should have accepted the dress I borrowed for you.''

There was a decided chill in her voice when the countess replied. ''I admit, Miss Harding, that my standards have slipped some during my travels, but I would like to disabuse you of the thought that I would stoop so low as to wear borrowed clothing. Furthermore—"

She stopped midsentence as they both strained to determine the cause of the commotion in the hallway outside their room. The countess, her hearing somewhat impaired by age and overindulgence, cupped her hand behind her ear. "What is it? Have the servants disposed to clack and gabble above stairs?"

"I don't know. I thought I heard someone shouting in alarm. A woman, I think. Perhaps we ought to see about it."

The countess pushed herself away from the table. "Indeed. I'll tend to it straightaway."

"But maybe we shouldn't interfere."

"Nonsense. I won't stand for such shocking behaviour."

Before Emily had a chance to stop her, the countess had flung the door open and was striding into the hall. There was nothing for Emily to do but follow in her wake.

The butler and three others, apparently members of the serving staff, were pounding and pulling at a small child who seemed to be in dire straits. It was clear from the shouts and screams that there was a state of panic and no one was in control. The countess descended on the group with arms akimbo and plucked the child from the butler's arms. Only then did Emily see that the boy's face had turned a dusky blue.

With one hand on the child's ankles, the countess upended him and swatted him smartly on his backside. A small round object popped from his mouth and he let go a bloodcurdling scream.

A woman grabbed the child away but the butler touched her arm. "It's all right, Maggie. See, young Michael can breathe now."

Maggie, who, Emily perceived, was the boy's mother, drew a long, shuddering sigh. "Aye, 'e can, can't 'e? She's gone an' saved 'is life, she 'as."

The countess patted the maid's shoulder. "It's nothing, my dear." She turned to the butler with a disapproving air. "Fredricks. Suppose you see to that sherry if you can spare the time."

"I believe I could do that, ma'am, if you ladies would like to step back into the reception room. Would you care for the dry or the sweet?"

"The dry. Spanish, of course."

The butler passed Emily a look. She shrugged. Never let it be said that the countess was unschooled in the bibulous arts.

As they returned to resume their wait, James Berrington came striding into the corridor just outside the doorway to the reception room. "Just what is going on here, Fredricks? Why aren't you at your post? Who are these people? What are they doing in my house?"

The countess seemed to devour him with her eyes. Then, in one giant stride, she was upon him, smothering him in her potent embrace. She held him at arm's length and searched his face. "James. James, my son! How I've longed for this moment. I knew I'd find you. I knew that we would be together once again."

His astonishment was profound. Emily watched the tableau with considerable enjoyment. The earl, of course, looked older than she remembered him. His jaw still had a familiar square set, but his dark hair now sported carefully trimmed sideburns, giving him a look of distinction.

As quickly as he could, he divested himself of the countess, stepped out of her reach, and brushed at his clothing with considerable disgust. "Who the devil are you, woman? And what manner of nonsense is this? Fredricks?"

CHAPTER TWO

FREDRICKS BUTTONED his coat and stood at attention, his chin tucked smartly into his collar. Only the movement of his eyes betrayed his harried emotions. "I beg your indulgence, milord. If I might speak with you alone, sir?"

The countess stiffened, swirling her ragged shawl over one shoulder in a great show of haughty contempt. "Really, James. You always were a bit of a prig, but not to recognize your own mother is beyond the pale."

James picked up the gloves he had thrown on the table and slapped them across his thigh. "What utter rubbish! What kind of charade is this? You are no more my mother than I am father to—to—" he stammered, "the statue of Jupiter standing in the front hall."

The countess rolled her eyes. "Hermes, James, not Jupiter. You never could keep the two straight."

James looked startled but quickly regained his composure. "And you." He turned to face Emily. "I suppose you are the Duchess of Heatherwood?"

Emily smiled slyly. "Really, sir, do I look that old? Suffice it to say that the duchess and I have chatted on occasion and I have been a guest in her house, but a closer relationship I cannot claim."

The countess looked surprised. "Friends with the duchess? My dear, I had no idea we had a mutual acquaintance. You never mentioned Elizabeth."

Emily grinned. "Well, I doubt that her grace has seen fit to mention me more than once or twice in the past ten years."

The earl was fast becoming vexed. "What is this? Teatime at Carlton House? Please be so good as to leave my house at once."

Fredricks cleared his throat. "Milord, there is something I must tell you."

"I've no argument there. Well, speak up. What is it?"

"A few minutes ago young Michael was stricken when a plum lodged in his throat. It was only this woman's quick action which saved him."

James stepped safely out of the countess's reach and grasped the front of his vest. He scrutinized the countess, then his gaze shifted to Emily for what seemed to her like an overlong appraisal of her face and figure. He frowned. "Indeed. I am sure we are most grateful. However, that does not explain this woman's presence in my home, not to mention her untoward behaviour."

The countess glared. "And why should I have to explain my behaviour? If anyone owes an explanation, James, it is you, for having acted towards your mother in such a cavalier fashion."

The earl looked as if he were ready to breathe fire.

Emily reached for her bonnet and pulled it snugly over her hair. "If you will permit me, your lordship, perhaps I can clarify the situation."

He set his jaw in a hard line and stared at her without speaking. She tucked a curl under her bonnet. "I daresay our visit has come as something of a surprise. It was the day before yesterday when I chanced upon the countess, who was being pursued and set upon by a gang of young toughs. She was exhausted and hungry and without funds, so I took her to my room for the night."

His voice was dry. "How decent of you. And now you plan to palm her off on me. And no doubt you will expect a reward for it, too."

"I believe I understand your discomfort, but you've no need to stoop to insults, my lord. Whether or not this woman is your mother I cannot say. It seems to me it should not be too difficult a thing to determine. As for me, I want nothing from you, nor would I accept any token or reward."

"We shall see, shall we not?" He snapped his fingers and spoke to a uniformed lackey. "Bring me the bag of coins from the drawer in the library." Then turning back to Emily and the countess, he inclined his head briefly.

"I can see that both of you are in need of some kind of protection, but your criminous behaviour tempts me to turn you over to the constables post-haste. However, out of gratitude for your having saved the boy's life, I see fit to be generous." He paced the floor, stopped for a moment to survey the countess, who leaned heavily against a chair, then clasped his hands behind his back and continued to pace.

When the servant returned with a small bag of coins, the earl took it and spread them out on the table in a gold cascade. "There. These should suffice to see you through for many months, providing you are judicious in the way you use them."

Neither of the women moved but Emily thought she saw the countess waver. Her eyes blinked twice and she appeared to catch her breath. The money would have been a fortune to the woman. Why didn't she take it and go?

The earl's mouth tightened as he refilled the bag with the coins, then tied the top securely with a thin length of leather. He held it towards the countess. "Take it. Take it and begone."

At first Emily thought the countess had reached for the coins, but instead she grasped her son's arm, opened her mouth as if to speak, then slid to the floor in a dead faint.

Emily rushed to her side and knelt down. "Quick, a vinaigrette." She looked pointedly at the earl. "Now, see what you've done. I told you she was exhausted. She's hardly breathing."

The earl looked sceptical. "I suppose this is part of the act. I credit you, both of you would do well on the stage. I'm almost convinced she has fainted." He motioned to the footmen. "Carry her into the library and place her on the settee."

The countess stirred and sat up, only to lean back against the wall. She looked as pitiful as a lost waif when the footmen helped her to her feet, but there was something in her eyes...something about the set of her chin which made Emily's hands shake. There was a resemblance. There truly was! For the first time she began to believe that the woman really was Lady Marguerite Carstairs, mother of James Carstairs, Earl of Berrington.

As she followed the shameful procession down the hallway, Emily's temper began to smoulder and her mood was reflected in her eyes as she met the earl's stony gaze. "Be advised, sir, if anything happens to your mother, I'll see to it that every newspaper in London gets wind of the scandal."

"By all that is holy! If you persist in calling her my mother, I'll be the first to give the scandalmongers something to write about. My mother is dead. Has been for nearly seventeen years. She perished at sea off the Italian coast. My father, as well."

Emily caught her breath and the earl saw her eyes widen. He felt a surge of satisfaction. At last he had succeeded in breaking her stride. It was obvious this adventurous young woman had not expected to be confronted with such indisputable truth. Confound it, it felt good to be in control of the situation again. It was a long time since anyone had come even close to besting him.

Emily's voice was unsteady. "Your parents dead? You can't mean that?"

"I most certainly do."

"Are you sure? I'm so sorry. But is it possible, sir, that there could have been some kind of mistake?"

His gaze narrowed. "Would it satisfy you if I showed you their gravestones?"

"Yes. Of course it would."

He shifted his feet and adjusted his neckcloth. "Well, I would, but naturally they were buried in Brighton."

Emily raised her eyes to the circle of plaster cherubs which adorned the ceiling. "Of course."

"Young woman, I don't like your tone of voice."

"Forgive me. It is only that I am so strongly convinced the countess truly is your mother." She pressed her hands together. "Won't you even consider that there could have been a mistake?" she asked gently.

His dark eyebrows drew together in a magnificent scowl. "Your imagination borders on the romantic."

Emily wasn't to be put off. "I suppose you're right, but how do you explain the fact that the countess knows this house? She knew where to find the key for the front gate. She knew about the statue of Hermes." Emily saw his look of disgust but she couldn't stop herself. "Tell me. The wallpaper in the salon. Is it Oriental in design?"

"Yes. Why do you ask?"

"And does it depict storks in a field of pale rose chrysanthemums and blue delphiniums?"

"Why yes, I believe it does, but—"

"And did your father and mother discover the wallpaper when they were touring the Orient? And were the draperies blue velvet before you changed them to burgundy?"

"Confound it, woman what you say is knowledge obtainable from any number of sources. It doesn't prove anything."

"It does to me. I think something happened back then." She studied his finely chiselled mouth, the square jaw. "Consider, my lord. Sixteen years ago you were a mere boy. You may have misunderstood the implications...."

"Enough! If you continue this miserable fabrication I shall have no qualms about bringing charges against the two of you. My mother is dead, I tell you."

"Then I apologize. If what you say is true, I would be the last one to expect you to take this woman under your protection."

"I would be a fool to do it, would I not?"

Emily shrugged. "Perhaps so. I have never heard you called foolish, your lordship. Nor can I recall that anyone has ever accused you of being overly charitable." She saw the irritation flash across his face but she plunged on. "Although you refuse to admit that Marguerite could be your mother, surely you could find it in your heart to let her stay here for a few days until she gets her strength back." Emily spread her hands in an encompassing gesture. "This huge house. You must have ten, fifteen bedrooms, not to mention the servants' quarters."

He smacked his forehead. "You put me in a damnably awkward position. But yes, I suppose, out of consideration for the fact that she saved young Michael's life, I could allow her to stay here for a few days."

Emily softened. "Thank you, your lordship. It's very good of you."

"Is it, indeed?" His voice resembled a growl. "Personally, I consider it just short of bird-witted to become involved in such a farce, but I have an appointment and no time to debate."

He signalled to two footmen. "You, Edgar, Jeeves, accompany the elder woman upstairs to the rose suite. Have Mrs. Grover send someone to help her undress."

The countess took in all this with a weak smile. "You see, Emily? I told you my son would remember me. James is such a dear boy."

Emily bent to squeeze her hand. "You'll be all right now, countess. Take care of yourself and allow your son a little time to adjust to your return."

James Carstairs swore softly. Emily straightened and curtsied in gratitude to the earl, then turned and started towards the door. He followed her and took her by the shoulder. "Not so fast, young woman. Where do you think you're going?"

"Back to my lodgings, of course. I need to rest so that I can look for work on the morrow."

"I think not."

"I beg pardon?"

"I will allow that woman to remain here on one condition, that you accompany her, look after her, and see that she stays out of the sherry. My present staff is not adequate to string-tie an elderly woman."

"I can't possibly remain here. For one thing, I have much to do. I must look for work. For another, the countess is a stranger to me. I only met her three days ago."

"Then you are one feather up on me, for I first set eyes on her not twenty minutes ago."

"Surely you don't expect me to believe that."

"Believe this, if you choose to leave now, you will take that impostor with you."

"Be reasonable, Lord Berrington. If it were within my means to care for her I would have done so in the first place rather than subject a mother to her son's disdain."

Emily looked around the corridor at the lavish display of tapestries, crystal chandeliers, and inlaid wood. "I can't begin to imagine what she must have done to you, my lord, to incur your utter disregard for her well-being. I could perhaps understand your unwillingness to admit to the relationship if you hadn't a pair of shillings to rub together, but you are without doubt a very wealthy man." Emily tied her bonnet strings neatly under her chin in preparation for departure.

"Surely your staff of servants is more qualified than I to look after her. If you are so reluctant to allow her to stay here, then you are doing her no kindness. And indeed, if she truly is your mother, she has my profound sympathy."

"Egad. Your tongue could put a rapier to shame. I don't know how you came to be involved in this miserable charade but I venture to say, miss, that when I learn the truth, I will waste no time in settling our account as well as giving you the setdown you so richly deserve."

His words, though a threat, seemed somehow to lack the sharp edge which she would have deemed appropriate, if he meant what he was saying.

Emily dismissed them with a soft voice and a gesture of her hand. "If it is your intention to frighten me, Lord Berrington, you have failed miserably. Now, if you'll excuse me, I bid you good-day."

She smiled, dropped a curtsy, lifted her chin, and sailed past him in the general direction of the grand entrance. Lord Berrington, watching her go, was left with mixed emotions. The chit was right, of course. He was a rich man. Whatever their game was, it could prove entertaining to best them at it.

His gaze followed her, dropping to the flash of trim ankles below the hem of her skirt and to the black slippers, which though of good quality, gave testimony to hard wear. What made her refuse the bag of gold coins? To someone like her it could have meant salvation. Yet she never hesitated. Was she manoeuvring for a better position in the hope of gaining even greater wealth? Of course.

"By Jove!" he swore softly. It wasn't like him to let a woman have the last word. He wouldn't let her get away with this. And it had nothing to do with the fact that she was a cut above the ordinary in her feminine appeal. It was the challenge which intrigued him, and her obvious intelligence.

She was a tad too sure of herself for one in her position, and a woman, at that. He would beat her at her own game and tie her up with her own bonnet strings. When it came to playing games he was quite unbeatable, and right now he needed something to rid himself of the malaise which had plagued his existence for the past two years.

Before he could change his mind, he strode swiftly down the corridor and intercepted her before she reached the front door. With his arm braced solidly against the doorframe he succeeded in blocking her way. "And just where do you think you are going?" he demanded, his voice deceptively smooth.

Emily stopped abruptly to avoid a collision. "I don't see that my destination is any concern of yours." She put her gloved hand on the sleeve of his coat. It was a foolish move on her part because it brought them into close confines, forcing her to look up into dark eyes which glittered dangerously. Her voice was none too steady as she pulled back. "Kindly remove your arm and allow me to pass."

James was shaken by the warmth of her touch on his arm. Even through the fabric he could sense the current of emotion which suddenly enveloped them. He came to attention, then bowed smartly in an effort to regain control. "Leave if you wish, madam. And be it upon your head when I cast the old woman into the streets immediately behind you."

"You wouldn't." He saw her falter and he managed to control his triumph.

He stood there grim-faced, with eyes as dark as the obsidian ring he wore on his right hand. Emily knew she was beaten. She leaned against the wall, pressing her hands against her cheeks.

His breathing slowed and he clasped his hands behind his back, feet spread wide in the attitude of a general about to address his troops. Although he didn't smile, there was a touch of humour in the set of his mouth.

Emily drew herself up sharply. "You like to win, don't you?"

He flicked at an imaginary piece of lint. "I don't know. There's nothing to compare it to. You see, I *always* win."

"Oh!"

"Well, speak up. What is your decision?"

Emily squared her shoulders. "It seems that I have little choice in the matter."

He inclined his head. "A wise decision. I hope that one of the first things you do is see that your friend is bathed and decently clothed. My housekeeper will choose some suitable gowns from the attic storeroom."

Emily laughed sharply. "That may be easier said than done, my lord. Once before I offered borrowed clothing to the countess, and she turned it down flat."

"Then I suggest you devise a way of getting round her, because I'll not have her in the house smelling as she does—like some gin-soaked hoyden."

"You ask a great deal of me, sir."

"*I* ask a great deal? Your sense of justice is a hair short of outrageous, but suffice it to say that the two of you must deport yourselves with some degree of civility or I shall see to it that you are both dispatched back to where you came from." He looked about him. "What has become of your luggage?"

Emily glared at him. "The countess had none. As for myself, I had no intention of remaining longer than it took to deliver your mother into your loving care."

"Sarcasm does not become you." He stroked his chin. "Very well. I'm sure we can find something for you to wear, provided you are not too particular." He ordered another footman to show Emily to the suite adjoining the one occupied by the countess. "Mrs.

Grover will see to your needs once she has finished with…confound it all, what am I to call the woman?''

"You might try calling her 'mother.'"

"Give me credit for at least a small degree of common sense." He saw the smile which Emily tried unsuccessfully to hide, and it amazed him to see how it sparkled in her eyes.

"Then perhaps you could call her 'Countess,' as I do."

"Not much of an improvement. We'll have to think of something more appropriate. And what am I to call you?"

Emily tensed. She didn't want him to know the complete story of her background. If he knew she was still under obligation to Mr. Grimstead, the earl might well send her back to him. Better to keep her title a secret until she could judge the full extent of her situation. She dazzled him with a smile.

"Why not just call me Mrs. Harding?"

"*Mrs.* Harding? You didn't tell me you were married." The disappointment was evident in his voice.

"Neither did you apprise me of your own marital status."

He blustered and a red flush crept up to his chin. "Confound it all. I saw no reason to."

"Quite right. Nor did I see any reason to present my own personal dossier." She fixed him with a softer gaze. "If it will make you less uncomfortable to know something about me, I must tell you that I am a widow. I lost my husband just over a year ago."

The thought occurred to James that she had probably killed the late Mr. Harding with her acid tongue, but he remembered his manners. "My condolences, madam. It was not my intention to distress you."

"Thank you, but I have come to accept my husband's death." Emily waited for him to give some clue to his own eligibility, but the silence was prolonged. Even though she assumed he was unmarried, common courtesy dictated that he oblige her. She stiffened. "If you have finished questioning me, my lord, I would like to retire to my room. The countess may need me."

"Of course." He motioned to the footman, then turned abruptly and strode down the hall.

The footman, impassive in his grey-and-black livery, bowed Emily in the direction of the stairway, which swept upwards in a wide curve towards a wall hung with a vibrant tapestry. The scene it depicted was of a stag leaping over a fallen log. In the background, the battlements of a castle sparkled white in the sun where they rose high above a forested glen.

Emily had had little opportunity to appreciate her surroundings since she arrived, except to note that the house was large and well-appointed. Now she became aware of the polished floors, the crystalline sparkle of chandeliers, the gleaming windows set behind filmy curtains of a rich ivory colour. In an age where velvet hangings were all the rage, the absence of heavy draperies in the entrance hall surprised and pleased her.

The footman directed her down a long hallway which was lighted at intervals by lamps set into niches or on tables next to the walls. At the far end of the hallway, an oriel window flooded the corridor with sunlight.

The footman stopped in front of a door, opened it, and motioned her inside. "This is the lilac suite, madam. It adjoins the rose suite which—" He paused, embarrassed.

"Her ladyship," Emily provided.

The footman's eyes twinkled. "Yes, ma'am. Which her ladyship has been given. If there is anything you wish, simply pull the bell cord which you will find next to your bed."

Emily thanked him and he closed the door after her.

The room was charming. Tall, narrow windows, their top sections mullioned and set with coloured glass in shades of lilac, pink, and deep purple, lined one wall. The lower two-thirds of the windows were of clear glass, which allowed one to look down upon the gardens and walkways leading to an arboured maze.

The canopied bed was on a raised dais upon which rested a circular rug of the finest wool Emily had ever seen. It took her less than a minute to kick off her slippers and luxuriate in the feel of it. The bed, with its silken coverlet which matched the pale shades of pink, purple, and ivory in the rug, was surprisingly soft. No straw-filled mattress here. She was tempted to curl up and sleep for an hour or two, but conscience prevented it. She must first look in on the countess. After all, the countess was her responsibility now, whether she wanted it or not.

In truth, living here for a while offered certain advantages. She would have a chance to rest and regain her strength. Mr. Grimstead would never dream of looking for her here. She was safe—for a while, at least. Safe, that is, if she didn't cross swords once too often with Lord Berrington.

"James Carstairs. Lord Berrington." She rolled his name across her tongue. The years had improved him. It was stimulating to match wits with him, even though their exchanges sometimes bordered on hostility. And she could hardly fault him for his reluctance to admit the possibility that the old woman might be his mother.

There had been a time when Emily and her husband were the target of the poor unfortunates who were forced to stoop to trickery to feed their families. But the money was gone now and she herself was among the needy.

She sighed. It wasn't the money she missed so much as the presence of an intelligent man in her home. She tried not to think about it. If nothing else, she had learned since Henry's death that each day must take care of itself.

Her room and the room the countess occupied were connected by a sitting room. Emily crossed to the opposite door with hardly a second glance at the richly patterned Aubusson rugs and the lustre of hand-rubbed woods. She tapped on the door and entered without waiting for a response.

A bug-eyed young maid, who identified herself as Millie, stood awkwardly near the bed. She shifted from one foot to the other. "Can you beat that, mum? I left long enough to fix 'er bath an' when I comes back to fetch 'er, she's dropped off." The maid edged away. "Maybe she up an' died on me. 'Eaven 'elp us, 'is lordship will 'ave me 'ide," she said, clasping her hands to her bosom.

The countess blew out her lips in an explosive snore. Emily laughed. "I don't think you have to worry, Millie. The countess is simply exhausted. Let's let her sleep for now. She has obviously been under a strain for a very long time."

"Aye, and she's a bit long in the tooth to be out on 'er own, so to speak." Millie squinted sideways at Emily's oft-mended gown. "Would you be wantin' to sleep, too?"

"Not now, thank you. You may carry the pitcher of water to my room and I shall refresh myself before I go downstairs."

"Yes, mum. Mrs. Grover told me to say that later today she will go through the armoires in the attic to see what she can find for the two o' you to wear."

"Thank you." Emily waited for Millie to move, but it was obvious that she had more to say. The maid's snapping black eyes expressed barely controlled curiosity. "Yes, Millie?" Emily asked. "Is there something else?"

"I was wonderin', mum, is it true what they say below stairs? Is she really 'is lordship's mother?"

"I think perhaps it would be best for you to save your questions until later."

"Indeed, mum. I meant no 'arm."

Emily managed to smooth things over without ruffling the maid's feelings. From the experience Emily had gained running her own extensive household before Henry's death, she knew how important it was to preserve harmony between master and servant.

A half hour later Emily looked in on the countess and found her still sleeping soundly. She tucked the coverlet more closely about her and then straightened to study the woman's face.

Was it possible that this woman was truly the earl's mother? If so, how did it happen that her body was supposedly buried in Brighton? Or was the earl simply creating a facade in the hope of tripping them up? She wouldn't put it past him. He wasn't an easy man. And yet—She furrowed her brow. There was something about him that intrigued her. His eyes were darkly compelling. One look from him made her feel vulnerable and childlike. But it was more than the way he looked at her, so much more. Instinct told her to guard against it. She had learned a great deal about the value of instinct in the days following her husband's death. Now that same instinct told her to leave quickly before she was swept far beyond her depth.

It was more than two hours later when Millie tapped at the door and told Emily that his lordship was waiting for her in the library.

Emily took one last look in the mirror and was dismayed by the paleness of her cheeks. She pinched them to bring up the colour, then followed Millie downstairs. On the way down they encountered Mrs. Grover, a tall, dignified woman who wore her responsibilities like a badge of merit. She greeted Emily with unsmiling respect, then continued up the stairs. Millie raised her eyes in a heaven-help-me look. It was ever the same between maids and housekeepers. Emily was hard put to keep from laughing.

The earl was poring over his account books when she knocked at the door. He scarcely bothered to lift his gaze from the paper. "So there you are, Mrs. Harding. Come in and sit down."

Emily was appalled by his lack of manners. "Don't bother to rise, my lord," she said with a decided chill in her voice. She made an elaborate curtsy before walking towards the chair which faced the table.

He had the decency to blush. "My apologies." He rose and bowed, then came round the end of the library table and held her chair.

Emily hesitated. "Perhaps you would prefer to speak to me a little later when you have finished with your work."

"No. I've ordered tea to be brought in." He clasped his hands behind his back and strode towards the hearth. A fire glowed darkly among the logs, infusing his face with light and shadow. It crossed Emily's mind that he looked half saint, half devil. She wondered which impression more clearly expressed his true character.

He rested one hand on the mantel. "I've been thinking about what I've got myself into. Having that woman here is sure to curdle the porridge unless I miss my bet."

"I'll grant that there are bound to be complications, but your mother, though a determined woman, does not seem the sort to ask for more than is her due. She told me she merely wants to end her days at home with the son she adores."

"Great smoking haystacks! Why in God's name did she have to choose me?"

Emily was amused by his boyish outburst. "I was under the impression that parents had little choice when it came to offspring. Nor do children have any say in choosing their parents." She grinned. "And a good thing, too, I suspect, or we'd all be nobles with no one to stoke the fire."

"Spare me the philosophy. You seem intelligent enough, Mrs. Harding. Assuming, perhaps wrongly, that you are not part of this outrageous flam, what must I do to convince you that this woman is an impostor?"

"And I say, sir, what must we do to convince *you* that she is not?"

CHAPTER THREE

HE WHIRLED ROUND and faced Emily with a look of profound exasperation. It took some doing, but he finally managed to control himself. "I warn you, Mrs. Harding, do not try my patience too far. I am willing to go along with this farce for a few days out of respect for the woman's age and infirmity, not to mention the fact that she saved young Michael's life." He stormed across the length of the room and back in great, sweeping strides. "What you fail to understand is that I have obligations. I find it convenient to entertain guests rather frequently, a fact which is difficult enough without a wife to handle such things. But just how am I to explain that... that woman to my friends and business associates?"

Emily felt an unexplainable surge of pleasure to hear it affirmed that he was unmarried. At the same time she chided herself for acting the fool. To hide her feelings, she picked up a glass paperweight and concentrated on the delicate lines of the carved primroses clustered within it.

"Why bother to explain her at all? The countess doesn't have to be included on the guest list. This house is so large she could easily confine herself to a separate wing."

"Be sensible, woman. Am I not correct in assuming that your friend is not one to isolate herself in a tower

room during festivities? One could hardly call her shy."
He picked up an ornamental snuffbox, then tossed it
aside in irritation. "I've not the slightest doubt that she
would plant herself right there at the head of the re-
ceiving line."

Emily laughed. "I fear you are correct, sir. And she'd
order her tiara brought out of the vault for even the
smallest event."

The image of the countess in her calico dress and
sagging stockings, with her thatch of grimy hair stick-
ing out from beneath a diamond tiara, was too much
for them. They looked at each other and burst into
laughter.

Emily pressed her hand over her mouth. "We should
be ashamed of ourselves for making sport of her. When
the countess is rested and bathed she may seem less—"

"Flamboyant?" the earl suggested.

"I had in mind something more in the way of..."
Emily sighed. "In truth, I cannot think of a word to
describe her."

"With good cause. She defies description." The earl
stroked his chin. "Of course we could provide her with
an ample supply of sherry to make certain she sleeps
through our parties."

"Your lordship!"

"Yes, yes, I apologize. There's nothing to be gained
by that. Besides, I venture to say it would take more
than half my wine cellar to put that one under the table
for long."

Emily glanced up to see if he was making a joke, but
there was no sign of laughter in his eyes. She folded her
hands into the long sleeves of her dress. "I'm sorry that
we have posed such a problem for you, yet I cannot
apologize for bringing your mother home. My instinct

tells me that in time you will come to admit she really is your mother.''

"I wouldn't place a wager on it if I were you.''

"My instincts have served me very well in the past.''

He studied the perfect oval of her face, so lovely and fair, yet so vulnerable-looking with the dusting of dark shadows beneath her eyes. "Forgive me, Mrs. Harding, but if you have such an uncanny ability to foresee the future, how does it happen that you have found yourself forced to seek employment in order to survive?''

She hesitated only a moment. "I did not claim to be perfect, my lord. One does not always have control of a situation, no matter how well prepared one is for the unexpected.''

"To that, Mrs. Harding, I can only say amen.'' He sensed a certain kinship with her at that moment and came round to sit on the edge of the table near her. "Have you any idea how many people come to my door in the space of a year, falsely claiming I owe them money? Or swearing that they have papers to prove they own a portion of my land? By all that is holy, wealth does not provide an easy ride.''

Emily made a tut-tut sound with her tongue. "My heart goes out to you, Lord Berrington. One has only to look at your wasted body and gaunt face to know how you've suffered all these years.''

His cheeks reddened. He rose abruptly and stalked to a globe that stood at an angle on a pedestal frame. His finger stabbed at it, sending it into a fast spin. "You needn't act so superior. I was not looking for sympathy.''

"Now it is my turn to beg forgiveness. It was inconsiderate of me. Though I didn't mean to sound quite so cruel, I find it hard to feel sympathetic towards one who dines on champagne and roasted quail and sleeps on silk sheets.''

He looked up slowly and his frown changed to a grin. ''Have you been sneaking into my bedchamber, Mrs. Harding? I consider it an honour, but suffice it to say that when I insisted you stay on to look after that—that woman, I didn't mean that you would also be required to see to my personal needs.'' He stroked his chin. ''Silk sheets, indeed.''

''Touché. It was merely a figure of speech, my lord. Suffice it to say that unless one has experienced poverty and pain one can scarcely imagine how destructive they can be to one's attitudes. Compared to what your mother must have gone through these past years, our troubles must be like a drop of rain in an ocean of water.''

''That may be true, Mrs. Harding, but since my mother is dead and buried I have no way of making it up to her.''

Emily was not convinced that his parents had passed on, and second thoughts reminded her that in any case he would doubtless stoop to trickery to prove a point. Nevertheless, she felt compelled to share his sorrow. ''If that is true, Lord Berrington, you have my sincere sympathy.''

''I'm overwhelmed.'' There was a certain dryness in his voice which even a fool could not miss hearing.

She rose and started to walk towards the door, but he stepped in front of her. Standing this close to him was like coming in from the storm on a winter's day. Although they did not touch, she sensed the warmth of his body and was drawn towards him. The thought sobered her and she looked up without smiling. "This conversation is leading us nowhere."

"On the contrary. I think we have made considerable progress."

"Indeed? In what way? You are no closer to admitting that the countess is your mother than you were from the moment you first saw her."

He laughed deep in his throat. "Admitting she is my mother would be fabrication, even insanity, but it could hardly be called progress. Progress in this sense means getting to know my adversary and defining my lines of defence."

Emily's eyes sparkled. "Ah! So you've decided to declare war."

"I doubt that it will come to war. This amounts to little more than a small skirmish, a battle or two, perhaps, but nothing so grand as war. The sides have been drawn, I grant you, but the victory is already mine."

He reached for her hands and held them in his palms as he looked deeply into her eyes. "I must confess that I shall miss these contests once I send you and that woman back to where you came from."

His thumbs drew a pattern over the palms of her hands and across her fingertips. He started in surprise as his fingers encountered calluses still too new to have healed. She winced, more from the reminder that she was the real impostor than from the pain of calluses caused by being an overworked seamstress.

He pressed her hands between his. "What is this? What happened to your hands?"

She drew away sharply. "It's nothing. Excuse me, please. It's time I looked in on the countess."

He sighed in exasperation. "You are quite possibly the most irritating woman I have ever met. There is so much you haven't told me. You're hiding something, I'm convinced of it. Something beyond this farce of resurrecting my mother."

His eyebrows drew together in a heavy dark line. "So why, in God's name, do I feel compelled to prove to you that this woman is not my mother, when it is the two of you who should offer proof?"

Emily folded her hands into her sleeves to prevent him from taking them again. Her voice was so soft that he had to strain to hear it. "Would you accept the proof if you saw it, your lordship?"

He laughed harshly. "Of course. But the water of the river could turn to gold before such proof could be found."

Emily looked wistful. "If only there were someone else who was present back then. You were but a boy, after all, when your parents died, but surely there is a relative who would remember your mother."

"All of them are gone now." He thought for a minute. "My mother had a younger brother, Spencer, who emigrated to the Colonies, but we lost touch many years ago. For all I know he may not even be alive now."

"There has to be someone. A solicitor, a friend?"

He frowned. "Now that you mention it, there *is* someone who should remember her. Hawkins Willoughby, our old gardener. I pensioned him off eight or nine years ago, but he still lives in a cottage near my country estate."

Emily's spirits lifted. "When can we call upon him?"

"It is nearly a day's journey from here. But perhaps it is worth the time it will take to sort this thing out."

"May we go tomorrow?"

He studied her face. "Perhaps the day after. Don't be too eager, my girl. When the truth comes out the game will be over for you."

She looked up at him and he was all but compelled to touch the dimple at the corner of her mouth. She lifted her chin. "Eager hardly describes the way I feel, my lord. This is the first time I've had the opportunity and pleasure of reuniting a mother with her only son."

The earl swore softly and would have grasped her shoulder, but she backed away just in time to avoid him.

"If there is nothing else, sir, perhaps I should retire to my rooms."

"Just as you wish," he said stiffly, then hesitated. "It is not my intention to restrict you to your rooms, Mrs. Harding. As a guest in my house you are welcome to enjoy the library and other common rooms, and of course you will join me for dinner. You, uh, seem to show an interest in the tapestries. If you care to investigate the ballroom on the third floor you will find an abundance of wall hangings as well as some fine paintings."

"That is kind of you, Lord Berrington. I assure you, you have been most gracious, and I don't wish to cause undue disturbance to your daily routine."

He looked at her for a long moment as if searching inside himself to find the right words. Then he bowed deeply and walked out of the room.

Emily was nonplussed. What a strange man. One moment he was ready to throw her into the street, the next, he offered her the run of his house. Was this part of his plan to throw her off guard in the hope that she would become so comfortable as to forget herself and reveal some dark plot?

Her face warmed. In truth she did find it necessary to maintain a certain control. Until such time as she decided to reveal her past, if indeed she ever did, she must carefully weigh her words as well as her actions. At the same time, she regretted the need to dissemble.

There was an indefinable something about James Elliott Carstairs which drew her to him in spite of the inner voice which warned her to keep her distance. He had, after all, told her in no uncertain terms that they were on opposite sides of a contest without rules. Knowing the kind of man he was, she wouldn't put it past him to use every advantage at his command. That could certainly include his not inconsiderable charm.

Emily pulled her shawl more closely about her as she left the library and climbed the stairs to the next floor. She had planned to go directly to her rooms, but the temptation to view the tapestries in the ballroom directed her feet across the landing to the stairway which led to the third floor.

Above her head, a domed ceiling set with thousands of cuts of stained glass cast splinters of coloured sunlight over her face and clothing, and she felt as if she were standing inside a fractured rainbow. It was breathtakingly beautiful. She walked on until she saw wide, double-arched doors which she assumed were the entrance to the ballroom.

They were slightly ajar. She stepped inside just in time to see a servant girl, draped in a white dust-cover against the chill, seat herself at the pianoforte and start to pick out a tune. Moments later she began to sing. Although her talent as a musician left much to be desired, her voice rang with a pure, controlled sound which filled the room with exquisite melody.

The girl could not be more than eighteen years old, Emily decided, although it was difficult to see beyond the impromptu cape. She wore a mob-cap of white with grey trim to match her uniform, and a thick braid of midnight-black hair hung down her back. The song continued as the girl, unaware of Emily's presence, continued to assault the pianoforte.

Emily stepped forward and touched her shoulder. "Wait. Let me play while you sing."

The girl jumped up so quickly that she banged her knee on the keyboard. She gasped something in French and then covered her mouth. "Madam, forgive me. I...I thought I was alone." Brown eyes widened in fear and her chin quivered. "Please don't tell on me. I promise I will finish the dusting at once." She wrung her hands. "What shall I do? His lordship will have my head on the guillotine for this."

Emily patted the girl's arm. "You have nothing to fear from me. You sing beautifully. I thought perhaps I might play for you." She smiled to put the girl at ease. "I am Mrs. Harding. And what is your name?"

The girl curtsied. "Yvette, madam. Yvette Corday."

Emily seated herself at the pianoforte. "I think I recognize the melody you were singing. 'Larks in the Autumn Rain,' is it not?" The girl was too numb to answer but Emily took up the song with unaccustomed fingers. At first she played slowly, willing her hands across the keys. Then as her fingers remembered the intricate glissandos, the music began to flow smoothly.

She glanced up at Yvette and nodded. Yvette gulped and began to sing in a quavering voice. But soon the music engulfed them and they worked together in fluid harmony.

When the song came to an end, they tried a few other well-known ones. Then Emily leaned back, saying, "There. We make a fine duet, don't you think? You have an exquisite voice, Yvette. Have you had musical training?"

"Oh no, madam." She gestured around the room. "I have my duties to look to— cleaning the marble, dusting, sweeping the carpets. There is no time for schooling."

"A pity."

"If there is nothing else, madam, I must finish my work before the evening meal."

Emily started. "Good heavens! I completely forgot the time. I must look in on the countess." She placed her hand on Yvette's shoulder. "Thank you for singing for me. Perhaps we could try again sometime."

"You won't tell Mrs. Grover? She would discharge me. I know that."

Emily was already at the door but she turned and called over her shoulder. "It's our secret. Never fear."

She was halfway down the corridor to the bedchamber when it occurred to her that she had led Yvette to assume that she, Emily, would be staying at the mansion for an indefinite period of time. It was impossible, of course, but it had slipped out so naturally. She must school herself not to succumb to the spell of this place and all it represented, for it would be far too easy to fall back into the role of lady of the house. And furthermore, she had not so much as glanced at the tapestries which graced the walls of the ballroom.

An ominous sense of disquiet struck Emily the moment she opened the door to her suite. Ordinarily she would have welcomed the silence, but her prolonged stay with Yvette played on her conscience and she hurried through the adjoining sitting room. When she opened the door to the countess's bedchamber, the bed was empty and the cover thrown back to the footboard. Marguerite's shabby shawl lay in a heap in the centre of the floor.

It was no use searching the room. Everything was in plain sight: a pair of cabriole chairs next to a table, a Queen Anne desk nestled in a small alcove, a massive armoire and a dressing table on the far side of the bed. Emily ran into the hallway and looked over the banister to the floor below, but there was no sign of the countess.

Her heart began to pound. Where was that woman? And what manner of mischief had she got herself into now? Emily leaned against the doorframe. *Stop. Think. Don't let yourself get rattled. The countess won't have left the house. All you have to do is find her.*

But that was easier said than done. Emily's first impulse was to search unaided for the missing countess, but her sense of privacy kept her from opening doors his lordship might have preferred left closed. A yank on the bellpull summoned Millie, who soon enlisted the services of the troop of footmen. They spread out over the house like, as Millie put it, "seeds from a dandelion on a windy day."

An hour later there was still no sign of the countess. No one had seen her, no one had heard her. The latter in itself was frightening, because the countess was not one to affect a well-modulated voice.

Lord Berrington chose that unfortunate time to return home. He summoned Emily to his side with undue haste.

"May I ask what precisely is going on? Not three hours ago I left this house a refuge of quiet, well-ordered serenity, only to return to find a veritable madhouse." Although he spoke softly, his words seemed to belie his apparent composure.

Emily dropped a brief curtsy, then folded her hands protectively into her sleeves. "I'm sorry, my lord. I regret having to tell you this but—but your mother is . . . missing."

A red flush suffused his face. "Missing, eh? For how long, if I may be so bold as to enquire?"

"I don't know for certain, but I think about three hours."

"Hmm. Then there is a good chance she has come to her senses and taken her leave. I'll warrant this is the best news I've had all week."

Emily shot him a cold look. "Your humour is ill-disposed, sir. It will be my fault if any harm comes to that woman."

"Your fault?"

"Of course. It was I who brought her here. You yourself gave me the task of looking after her."

"Indeed, from what I've seen of her demeanour, I think you need worry less about her and more about the havoc she might wreak upon my household." He massaged the back of his neck. "Have you searched the wine cellar?"

Emily raised her eyes heavenwards. "Twice, my lord. We've gone over the entire house. I've even sent some men to scour the grounds and the stables."

James saw that Emily was more overset than he had realized. He took her arm and motioned her to a chair. "Perhaps a glass of brandy would settle your nerves."

"No, I—"

She was interrupted by the butler, who entered, clicked his heels, and bowed. "Milord, the countess has been found."

Emily jumped up. "Is she all right?"

"Yes, madam. No harm has come to her."

The earl looked vastly relieved. "Then where the devil did she get to?"

"She was found in the attic, sir. Quite a sight she was, if I may say so."

Lord Berrington swore softly. "Now how in the name of all that's holy did she find her way up there?"

"We wondered the same thing, sir. Pulled the stairs up after her, she did. That's why it took so long to find her."

Emily started to the door. "Take me to her at once. I must see for myself that she is unhurt."

The butler led them up two flights of stairs, then down a maze of corridors to a storeroom with orderly shelves set on three sides. The fourth wall supported a very narrow folding stairway which was now firmly locked into place by a wooden pin. Fredricks motioned upwards. "You'll find her up there, but I'd be careful, mum. The steps are none too steady."

James stepped in front of Emily. "Wait here. I'll climb up and bring her down."

"I'll do no such thing."

James shrugged and motioned her to precede him.

The countess sat enthroned on an ancient gilt settee amidst furniture, statues, paintings, rows of trunks, and boxes enough to ballast a large sailing vessel. On her head was a monstrous purple hat with veils and ostrich feathers which reached down to her knees. She was sorting the contents of a small chest.

Apparently she heard them approach because she tilted back her head and looked down her nose. "Oh James, dear, it's you. I've just been looking at some of the mementoes from your childhood. They bring back such lovely memories. Like this wooden harlequin with the movable limbs."

Emily saw James's eyes narrow. His voice had an edge when he spoke. "I remember the day my father carved it for me."

The countess blustered. "Your father was all thumbs, my dear. It was Hawkins Willoughby, the gardener, who carved it for you on the occasion of your fifth birthday." She fished in the box. "But your father gave you this silver whistle in the shape of a bird. You used to wear the chain around your neck. You drove us nearly mad trying to mock the birds, as I recall."

Emily looked at James and was pleased at his expression of discomfort. She nudged him and whispered, "Does that tell you something? Or is the countess simply making up things as she goes along?"

"Anyone could have come by the information. It proves nothing."

He had made no effort to keep his voice down, but if the countess heard him she chose to ignore it. She put the box on a table and stood up. As she did so the sari of brilliant orange and purple silk flowed out about her. The ensemble of sari and feathered hat was outrageous.

The countess saw Emily's barely controlled mirth and shrugged. "Yes. Ridiculous, isn't it? But it brings back such memories. My husband brought it from India along with a trunk full of silks and spices and brass pieces." She took off the sari and stood once more in her calico rags. "But there was one gown, a blue-and-silver brocade that I particularly liked, and I'll be dashed if I can find where they've put it."

Lord Berrington frowned. "You shouldn't be up here. It isn't safe. The wood in the floor has not been completely reinforced, and it could give way if you're not careful where you tread."

"Fiddle! Your great-grandfather built this house of the finest woods available. It will outlast us all."

Emily took her arm. "I was worried about you, countess. Will you come downstairs now?"

Before the countess could protest, James took her other arm and steered her towards the stairs. "Mrs. Harding is right. Cook will soon have our evening meal ready and she hates to be kept waiting."

The countess sniffed. "In my day it was the master who gave orders, not the other way round." She pulled away. "Very well, if you insist. Fetch that box of gowns and underpinnings. I'll send the housekeeper up to search for the silver brocade. I can't understand what they could have done with it."

James gave Emily a helpless look and did as he was told.

Once they had the countess safely installed in her room under the careful ministrations of the maid, who was given orders not to let her out until she was scrubbed clean, Emily drew James into the corridor. "Can you still deny, sir, that this woman is your mother? How else could she know all these things?"

He grasped the ends of his waistcoat. "I admit that she makes a good case for herself but—"

"But? How can there be any question that she is who she claims to be? She found an all-but-secret stairway to the attic. She knew things about your childhood which even you had forgotten." Emily spread her hands in a gesture of frustration. "The proof is there if you are but willing to admit it."

"I admit nothing."

Emily laughed, and he was enchanted by the way her laughter drifted like the sound of silver chimes down the hallway. He crossed his arms in front of him. "I admit nothing," he repeated, "because there is nothing to admit. Not a word of what she said is true."

"There was no blue-and-silver brocade?"

He looked away and let out his breath in a long sigh. "I wouldn't know about the dress. I certainly can't remember having seen one like it."

"And the sari?"

He shrugged. "I admit only that my father did at one time travel to India."

"And the carved harlequin?"

"Aha! There I have you, madam. She was wrong. In truth it was my father who carved the toy, not old Willoughby. And it was for my fourth birthday, not the fifth."

His face was so delightfully animated that Emily found it hard to press a serious argument. She tucked a stray curl into place and regarded him with amusement. "Surely you must know that her age could account for a slight distortion of events."

She clasped her hands together as she warmed to the subject. "Ah—and how about the whistle?" she asked. "Was the countess wrong about that?"

The earl was silent for a moment, then reached into his pocket and extracted a silver bird strung on a delicate chain. "Is this what you mean?"

"How should I know? Is it a whistle?"

He held it to her mouth. "Blow."

She did as he instructed and was rewarded with a trill of musical notes. Before she could say anything, he took it from her and put it to his own lips and gently blew a few notes.

His eyes darkened with an intensity which shortened her breath. She knew he wasn't thinking of the bird-song. As clearly as if he had said so, Emily knew that the whistle was still warmed by the taste of her own mouth.

CHAPTER FOUR

EMILY LOOKED quickly away from the intensity of his gaze. "Excuse me," she said, trying unsuccessfully to calm her shaking voice. "I must see to the countess."

The earl slowly lowered the whistle from his mouth and twirled it from the end of the chain. "As you wish." It occurred to him that something had passed between them, some indefinable intimacy which caused his heart to beat more quickly. Before he could pursue the thought, the housekeeper came into the hallway with her arms full of clothing.

"Begging your pardon, madam, I've gone through the armoire and found a few dresses and such which might be suitable for you." She sniffed. "The other woman has already seen fit to oblige herself of a number of gowns from the attic."

Emily was embarrassed. "I hope she hasn't overstepped herself."

The earl guffawed. "If you are so firmly convinced that she is the countess, then why would you assume it would be possible for her to overstep herself? If she is indeed the countess, then she would have no reason to beg permission for anything she might choose to do." He chuckled, then smoothed his hand across his cravat. "Is it possible, madam, that there is a chink in the armour of your trust in this woman?"

"Not at all," Emily assured him, although she knew in her heart that there was one small glimmer of doubt. The real countess was, according to reports, dead and buried in a grave in Brighton, was she not? With all the evidence to the contrary, one could hardly support the belief that she had suddenly returned. But not for a minute would Emily admit her misgivings to James.

Mrs. Grover shifted the clothing to her left arm. "Excuse me, milord. There's one other thing you might like to know. I found the blue and silver brocade dress what that woman was looking for. In the trunk it was, wrapped in a velvet manteau."

James thanked the woman with a singular lack of warmth.

Emily smiled broadly and dropped a curtsy. "Excuse me, Lord Berrington. I really must attend to the countess." Without waiting for his response she turned abruptly and followed in the housekeeper's wake.

James watched her as she sailed majestically down the hall. "I'll expect you to join me for sherry in the library at seven, Mrs. Harding," he called after her. "You might try on one of those gowns for size. Anything would be an improvement over what you are wearing."

She stopped dead in her tracks and turned to give him a look which would have withered an oak tree. When he grinned at her, she raised her chin and continued towards the stairs.

James lifted the silver whistle and blew a series of trills which echoed down the hollow corridors past closed doors. A childish thing to do, but it made him feel good. It was exciting to cross swords with her once more. Much safer than letting himself be swept away by urges which he knew would become increasingly difficult to control. If he were going to win at this game, he would certainly have to be on guard.

He shoved the whistle into his pocket and hurried downstairs to his bedchamber, where he called for Chesney, his manservant, to begin laying out his clothes. On guard, yes. Then why was he so impatient for the hands of the clock to point to seven?

EMILY, TOO, FOUND herself watching the clock, but she laid her impatience to the fact that most of the gowns were too large for her. If she were to find something to wear to dinner, she would have to stitch it in at the waist and bodice.

With Millie's help she finally selected a gown of muted rose, which fell to the floor in a straight line from just below the bodice. The hem was embroidered with a wide band of flowers in shades of pink, violet, and pale yellow, interspersed with leaves of moss green. There was an ivory-handled fan to match the softly flowing gown, as well as slippers and unmentionables which smelled faintly of cedar.

Emily stood still while Millie bit off another length of thread. "Just one more little tuck, mum, and then we'll 'ave a look."

"It's a lovely gown," Emily said. "I wonder to whom it belonged."

"I couldn't say, mum. Nothing's been touched in the attic since I've been in the earl's employ."

"Have you been here long?"

"Aye, nearly seven years now." She paused while she applied the needle to the gown and began to stitch the tuck in place. "'Is lordship saved me from the bagnios, he did. I was down on me luck when George, me 'usband, a real bedpresser 'e was, was dragged off to sea."

"How terrible. You must miss him dreadfully."

"No, mum, I can't say as I do. 'E never was much good. A sure enough crack-rope kind o' man but 'e kept me in bread. I credit 'im for that, though now that I looks back, I'd guess what little 'e 'ad was filched from someone else. Truth is, I'm better off now than I ever was."

Millie pulled the thread through and knotted it before breaking it off. "There, now." She rocked back on her heels and smiled widely to reveal considerable space between her front teeth. "If I may say so, mum, you look pretty enough to be groom bait."

Emily laughed. "Thank you, but I'm not looking for a husband." She walked to the Empire mirror which stood in the corner of her room and surveyed herself with a critical gaze. "You've done a good job, Millie. It's a very long time since I've looked quite so presentable."

Millie cocked her head. "Since before your 'usband died?"

Emily looked surprised, then remembering how quickly news spread along the servant grapevine, she smiled. "Yes. Since Henry left me a widow."

"Well, don't worry yourself, mum. With your prospects, you won't remain a widow for long."

Emily picked up a silk scarf and drifted it across her shoulders. "Prospects? I have no money, nothing."

Millie came over to stand next to her and their gaze met in the mirror. "Lord love us, with your looks you don't need money. Forgive me, mum, but you ain't foolin' no one. You're no menial. Even a ninnyhammer would know that you must be a noble. Down on your luck maybe, but a noble, all right."

Emily moved quickly towards the table and picked up her fan. She passed it in front of her face several times before she spoke. "Have you discussed this with anyone else?"

Millie had the decency to blush. "We meant no 'arm, mum, but servants talk. And we 'ave to look after what's best for 'is lordship. 'E's a good man, 'e is, for all 'is stiff ways. If anyone was apt to cozen 'im, we wouldn't stand for it."

"Then you are to be commended. If it will put your mind at ease, Millie, I have no wish to remain here any longer than necessary. I have my own life to contend with and it has nothing to do with Lord Berrington."

Millie seemed to regain her self-assurance. She laughed. "Beggin' your pardon, mum, but we've 'eard the two of you goin' at each other like two cats on the back fence. My sainted mother used to say that fightin' and backbitin' is a rope that pulls one straight to the altar."

Emily realized that she had spoken too openly with Millie, who was little more than a stranger. She tried to regain a modicum of control. "Your mother couldn't be more wrong this time. I would appreciate it if you and the others would avoid further speculation on the subject." She snapped her fan shut and gestured towards the door. "Would you be so good as to see if the countess is dressed and ready to go downstairs?"

"Yes, Mrs. Harding." Millie bobbed a curtsy and went into the other room.

If Emily had sincere doubts about the countess, they all but disappeared when she saw Marguerite a scant ten minutes later.

"Well, don't stand there like a buffoon," the old woman said. "What did you expect? All I required was a bath and someone to dress my hair. What do you think? Is the style too dated?''

"You look elegant. A little thin, perhaps, but the blue-and silver tiered brocade quite becomes you.''

"A little bare without my jewellery, but James doesn't see fit to hand it over." She sniffed and patted the lace-edged fichu. "That's filial gratitude for you. After all I've done for the boy.''

"Yes. Perhaps we should be going downstairs. His lordship is expecting us.''

The countess leaned back her head and looked down her nose. "You turned out reasonably well, my girl. Turn round. Hmm. Yes, we'll have something done about your hair." She clapped her hands. "Well, come along. James becomes testy if he's kept waiting.''

It was all too evident that the earl had been pacing the floor when the butler announced Emily and the countess. He looked up, then appeared to step back and make a longer appraisal of the two women. The transformation had obviously taken him by complete surprise.

Emily curtsied demurely, then spoiled it all by grinning up at him. "My lord, the countess looks rather well, don't you think? It's remarkable how perfectly the gown seems suited to her.''

He grunted. "A bit large on top, wouldn't you say?''

"I'll grant you that she is rather thin, but one can attribute that to the hardships she has endured these past years.''

"I—''

The countess interrupted him. "Well, don't just stand there acting moon-witted. See to the sherry, James. And I'll thank you not to discuss me as if I were some menial standing at attention.''

In spite of the grim set of his mouth, which showed his misgivings, he bowed deeply and motioned to the footman to serve the ladies. His own glass, still untouched, rested on a stool next to a gilt-embossed pedal harp. He picked up the glass, downed the sherry in a single gulp, and winced. Seeing the women bathed and dressed in decent clothing cast another light on the game they were playing, and he began to wonder if perhaps he had got in beyond his limit. Was it possible to take two women of questionable heritage and turn them into ladies in a matter of hours. *No.* More likely his earlier thought hit the mark, that they were actresses playing calculated roles for financial advantage. His only hope of learning the truth was to play along with them until he could catch them in a mistake.

Emily tried unsuccessfully to read his thoughts. There was no doubt that he was taken aback by the change in their appearance. His gaze kept returning to her, then moved away when she looked up at him. Her appearance had certainly changed, but it went deeper than that, for when she donned the rose silk it was as if she had put aside the year of poverty. She felt protected once again. Her natural dignity, which she had been forced to suppress while she worked as a seamstress, now surfaced in everything she did.

The countess behaved equally well—until her second sherry. When she finished it off and appeared to be ready for a third, the earl stood and cleared his throat. "I believe it is time for us to go in to dinner."

The countess put her hand to her ear. "Indeed? I didn't hear Emmet announce dinner."

"It's Fredricks, not Emmet. Emmet left our service many years ago."

"Humph. Such ingratitude. He was always treated with respect. Very well, let us proceed. Give me your arm, James. Emily, you follow behind, my dear."

James sighed and did as he was ordered.

Dinner went surprisingly well. It was served in a small dining room, with heavy silver and fine linens set atop a cherry-wood table. Although there were no flowers, a fact which the countess quickly pointed out, candle-light softened the room with flickering shadows.

The only uncomfortable moment was when the countess mentioned that the room seemed smaller than she remembered it. The earl's face froze. Then he ex-plained in a tight voice that a sliding wall had been in-stalled to divide the large dining room into two rooms for less formal occasions.

Emily gave him a significant look, which caused James to flush uncontrollably. He acknowledged, if only to himself, that seeing her dazzling smile was al-most worth a measure of personal discomfort. For most of the evening he forgot his vow to trap her into telling the truth and, instead, concentrated on entertaining the women with witticisms calculated to make them laugh.

Whether because of the seven-course dinner with its heavy foods and accompaniment of wine, or simply her advanced age, the countess had considerable trouble keeping her eyes open once the diners returned to the library. She was seated in an upholstered chair next to the fireplace, and in no time her head bobbed to her shoulder and she drifted off to sleep.

Emily was at a loss for something to do with her hands. A special kind of intimacy enveloped the two of them, now that the countess was asleep. It was as if the food and wine and excellent service had conspired to draw them into a circle of domesticity. A glowing fire in the fireplace added to the feeling of home which encircled them.

Emily needed to break the spell. She rose and walked over to the harp. "What a lovely instrument." Her fingers traced the carved column topped by a Cupid holding wreaths of scrolled flowers. The sound-board was painted in the style of Vernis Martin, with depictions of mythological characters playing musical instruments. She turned towards James. "It's by Cousineau of Paris, isn't it?"

"Yes. Made in 1780. It was a gift from the Duke of Wellington."

She trailed her fingers across the strings in a ripple of sound. James came to stand beside her. "Do you play?" he asked.

"A little."

"Would you play something for me? It's been a very long time since we've had music in this room."

She detected a note of regret in his voice and it occurred to her that he was not nearly so self-possessed as he pretended. Emily unclasped the fan dangling from her wrist and handed it to him. "I would love to play for you, though I must confess I am dreadfully out of practice." She seated herself on the round stool, then unconsciously arranged her gown in a fetching manner. "What would you like to hear?"

"Whatever you would like to play."

She paused for an instant with her hands resting on the strings and then began to play. The music floated out over the room like a canopy, enfolding them in silken cords of sound. James thought he recognized the music as a passage from a Beethoven symphony. He paced the room slowly, stopping from time to time to watch her. A candelabra set on a tall pedestal cast a halo of radiant light around her hair and face. James was entranced. He wanted the moment to go on forever, but at the same time some inner voice warned him. He swore softly and whirled, placing his hands on her shoulders none too gently, then turned her until she was facing him.

"Enough, madam. It's time you answered my questions. Just who the devil are you?"

Emily stiffened. "I don't know what you mean."

"Your act has gone far enough. I see through your charade and I'll not be bamboozled any longer."

"Kindly unhand me, sir."

James studied her face for a moment, then dropped his hands to his side. His eyes were obsidian-dark beneath heavy brows and his voice resonated with the intensity of his feelings. "Be warned, Mrs. Harding, I'll not permit you to leave this room until I know your true identity. Do you think me a fool? Do you think I'm some bumbling drazel without sense enough to know a woman of Quality when I see her?"

Emily rose from the stool and smoothed her skirt with shaking hands before raising her eyes to meet his gaze. "I assure you, Lord Berrington, that you have more than earned my respect for the consideration you've given your mother under these trying circumstances. I know how hard it must be for you to accept her after all these years, but I do not in any way confuse your doubts about her with stupidity. From all I have heard, you are a man known and admired for your intelligence."

He appeared to soften for a brief instant, then his mouth tightened and he swore softly.

Emily's eyes widened. "Please guard your tongue, sir."

"You are clever, Mrs. Harding, but flattery will not suffice. I'm waiting for your answer and this time I want the truth."

"Are you saying that I have lied to you?"

"Don't bandy words. You will have to tell me eventually, as you well know."

Emily sighed. There was truth in what he said. If he learned about her debt to Mr. Grimstead she would be in dire straits, but hardly worse off than she was before. She would have to chance revealing a partial truth.

"Very well, if you insist. My name is Emily Harding."

A muscle tensed in his jaw. "Kindly don't stop there."

"I . . ."

"Go on, Mrs. Harding. I'm waiting."

Emily folded her arms in front of her. "My husband was Henry Chatsforth Harding, Earl of Wallingford."

James slapped his hand smartly against his thigh. "So! I was right all along. You are here under false pretences. You lied to me, Mrs.—er, Lady Wallingford."

"Indeed I did not! It is true I may have dissembled, but not once did I prevaricate." She turned away from him and walked towards the window to look out on the garden, dimly illuminated now by flickering torches. "Since Henry was taken to his rest I have found it necessary to provide for myself. I found it advisable to forgo my title in the marketplace, for it is worse than foolhardy to flaunt one's rank among those who resent the nobility."

"Hmm. You mean he left you penniless?"

"Indebted, to be precise."

"The cad. Gambled it away, did he?"

"Certainly not! Henry was a good husband, as well as an honourable man." She traced her finger along the lead pattern which divided the panes of glass. The memories were almost too painful to consider.

"Then why—"

Tears sprang to her eyes. "Why? Because for two years Henry was dreadfully ill. It took all of our money, everything we had, to search for a cure, but as it was, we gained only time."

He came to stand beside her. "You poor thing. How you must have suffered." He was close enough to her that he could smell the fragrance of her freshly washed hair. Neither of them spoke until at last he touched her shoulder. "And then what happened? You were forced to give up your home. You came to live in London?"

"Yes."

"You said it was a year since your husband died? How did you live? Did your friends take you in?"

"No. I could never ask it of them." She remembered how the ranks had seemed to close against her after Henry's death. But could she blame her erstwhile friends? They had had their homes to think of and husbands whose eyes were apt to wander. She pressed her palms together. "It wasn't easy being on my own under those conditions, but I managed. I found work for a time but it…it ended and now I must look again."

"What kind of work did you do? Surely you were untrained in the trades."

She stiffened, fearing that he would discover she was running from Mr. Grimstead. "I assure you, Lord Berrington, I am not completely lacking in skills. I was able to take care of myself."

James had a sudden vision of Emily destitute and alone. The image sent a surge of heat through his body and at the same time he was repelled. His voice was harsh. "Yes, I suppose a woman as beautiful as you are would not delay long in finding a suitable protector."

Emily's first impulse was to strike him, but instead she pushed both hands against his chest with as much strength as she could muster. "Pray do not judge me by the standards you set for yourself, sir. You are a cad to suggest such a thing, and I do not take your presumption lightly."

He seized her wrists and held them tightly as he stepped quickly to maintain his balance. "Indeed, my words were ill thought out." His large, yet surprisingly elegant hands slid down from her wrists to grasp her fingers. "Once again I must beg your forgiveness. I remember the circumstances under which we met and I tend to forget my manners."

Emily attempted to pull away, but he held her hands firmly in his. Their strength was somewhat unsettling, as was the hint of spicy scent that clung to his waistcoat. She schooled herself to resist the pull at her senses and countered with a scathing retort. "Am I to understand, then, Lord Berrington, that your good manners are reserved for those of noble birth?"

"Hardly. The king's nod assures recognition, not respect. I have known bootblacks and scullery maids worth more than a dozen of those who rule them. I give them my respect as well as my friendship." His eyes narrowed. "But I hasten to add I waste no niceties on those who try to flam me, be they noble or serf."

He turned her hands palms upwards. "Common sense tells me that you are holding something back, Lady Emily. And, trust me, I will find out what it is." His eyes darkened. "If nothing else, I am a good judge of people. From the moment you arrived here I knew you were not as you pretended.''

She struggled again to free her hands, but he tightened his grip. In spite of herself, she was enjoying this proximity to danger. Yes, danger. For the first time since Henry died she was beginning to feel stirrings within her. It would be worse than foolhardy to allow herself to become sentimental over this man. As a widow of reasonably acceptable appearance she was fair game to most men who danced to the tune then cheated the piper. Without the blunt to back up her looks and her title, it was tacitly understand that she was a losel. Emily would rather avoid temptation than end up empty, brokenhearted, and alone.

She looked up at him, and the entreaty in her eyes shamed him so that he let her go. She moved backwards, clasping her hands behind her to still their shaking. ''As I recall,'' she said, ''you accused your mother and me of being actresses, or worse. By now you should realize you couldn't have been more wrong. If you are such a competent judge of character, you must surely know that the countess is telling the truth. As for me, what have I to gain by pretending?''

He stuck out his lower lip and rocked back on his heels. ''You are here, aren't you? A guest in my house? Sharing my fireside, eating my food, drinking my wine?''

Emily looked down at the borrowed dress. ''And wearing your gown?'' She gave him a dry look and they both burst out laughing.

When she recovered, she poked his chest with her forefinger. ''Admit it, your lordship. I am here at your suggestion. No, that is too mild a word. Your *command* is a far more apt description.''

His eyes sparkled with high good humour. "Very well. I consent to the fact that I coerced you into staying here, but you must in turn admit that you do not completely despise your surroundings. Or your host," he added softly as if in afterthought.

Emily sucked in her breath. "If... if truth be served, as it must, I can truly say that I admire this house and all of its furnishings."

"And?"

She feigned a look of puzzlement. "Was there something else, my lord?"

"Lady Emily, you are enough to try the patience of—"

He was interrupted by an explosive snore from the countess, who sat bolt upright in her chair. "Did I hear someone offer sherry?" she asked.

Lady Emily and Lord Berrington, having forgotten that she had dropped off some time ago, were both startled. Emily took swift advantage of the interruption. "No more sherry, Countess. The servants are finished for the night. You must have been dreaming."

"Perhaps I was. I thought I heard angels strumming their harps."

James looked at Emily and winked. "It seems you've been elevated from actress to angel."

Emily lifted her gaze to the ceiling in a gesture of helplessness. "Like mother, like son. I can see where you inherited your ability to assess character."

The countess attempted to rise, but she was stiff from having been seated at an awkward angle while she slept. Lord Berrington took her arm to assist her and she gave him a loving pat on the cheek.

"My dear boy. How good it is to be home with you once more." She shook out the folds of her skirt and

walked over to an ornate wooden panel which decorated one end of a bookcase.

"If memory serves me right, there should be a decanter of sherry and some glasses behind this carving."
She pressed a concealed latch and a door sprang open
to reveal tiers of neatly stacked glasses. "Indeed!
Where's the sherry? Did Emmet forget to stock the
cabinet, or has someone been nipping at the wine behind his back?"

Emily gave James a significant look that said, *aha—
one more brick to add to the wall of proof.* He returned the look with a helpless shrug, then went to stand
close behind the countess.

He spoke with surprising gentleness. "Emmet has not
been with the family for many years, madam. It's
Fredricks who stocks the shelves. Since I rarely see fit
to indulge at this late hour, I see no reason to keep a
supply of wine so close at hand."

She sniffed. "Just like your dear father, Lord rest his
soul. He was completely lacking in the finer graces of
hospitality." She reached up and chucked him under the
chin. "Never mind, my dear. Your mother's come home
to look after you."

She turned and walked away, but as she did so, a
thread at the bottom of her skirt caught under the sole
of James's boot. The countess let out a shriek as the
hem of her skirt gathered in a tight hobble around her
ankles.

James glanced down at the thread, entangled now on
a silver boot buckle. "Just a moment. I see the problem." He bent over and pulled sharply. As he did, the
entire hem of the garment unravelled, leaving the
countess standing in a gown that was several inches too
long for her.

"Drat that maid," she said, hitching up the dress and trying to look dignified. "I told her to knot the thread more carefully."

Emily stood with her hand over her mouth, her eyes riveted on the colour and fabric of the countess's dress. There was no doubt in her mind that the dress was the blue-and-silver brocade the countess had described. But neither was there any doubt in her mind that the real countess must have been several inches taller than the woman before them. She looked over at James and their gazes met and locked. As surely as if she could read his mind she knew his thoughts were on a parallel with hers. This woman could not be his mother. It was only a charade after all.

CHAPTER FIVE

JAMES GLANCED QUICKLY at Emily, then back towards the now apparent impostor. He would have made some disparaging remark to underscore his contention that the woman had attempted to dupe him, but when he looked again at Lady Emily he bit back the words. Her face showed a mixture of disappointment, disbelief, and sorrow. The advantage was his now, but seeing the pain so evident in her eyes, he drew himself to attention and half bowed.

"Ladies, the hour is late." He turned to the countess. "If you will permit, madam, I shall summon Millie to see you to your rooms."

She pursed her lips, then swished her skirt around in order to get the cumbersome thing under control. "Yes, a good idea, my boy. I do find that I am extraordinarily tired."

Emily tried to compose herself, but with obvious difficulty. "I will take the—the countess to her room, my lord. There is no need to summon the maid."

James laid his hand on her arm. "Stay. I wish to speak to you."

"Why does that come as no surprise?" Emily said dryly.

James reached over to pull the bell rope and the corners of his mouth tilted upwards. "For once our minds seem to work towards the same end."

"I fear I am forced to agree."

A short time later, after the footman and Millie had lent their support to steady the countess on her way upstairs, James confronted Emily. "Now, Lady Emily. It seems the charade is over and I was right all along. The woman is an impostor, albeit a capable one."

"I believed her. I was so sure."

Emily looked so soft and vulnerable that James felt his determination to be firm melt like so much snow on a summer's day. "I can well understand how you were taken in." He came to stand close beside her and Emily could feel the unwelcome awareness stir in her blood. His voice became husky. "Now that it is over, I must admit there were times when I, myself, began to entertain the thought that she might be telling the truth."

Emily was surprised. "I would never have guessed. You seemed so adamant, so sure of yourself."

He nodded. "Perhaps because I wanted it to be true, there were times when I wondered if she really could be my mother come back from the dead. But my intuition told me there was no true bond between us, and I do believe and trust in cognition, at least to a certain degree."

"You trust your intuition, yet you thought that I was a part of the charade? Do you still think that I, as well as the countess, was trying to dupe you?"

He gave her a droll look. "If truth be told, Lady Emily, you were not straightforward. You led me to believe that you were nothing more than a menial until you were confronted with the truth. As it is, I know that you continue to withhold something from me, though I have not the least idea what it is or why you mistrust me so much that you are unable to confide in me."

He waited, hoping the answer would be forthcoming, but she looked up at him with wide, unblinking eyes and slowly shook her head. Then her lashes lowered and his senses alerted. He watched her closely as she looked away and began to fiddle with the panniers of her skirt.

"Surely my life story can be of little interest to you. We have only just met, have we not?"

"Just met? Why, of course." An alarm went off in his head and it was as if a spark had ignited. *Emily.* The name had a familiar ring. He had personally known only one or two women by that name in his entire lifetime. Emily Jannsen, the wife of the Swedish ambassador, and Emily Latterby, a woman who had emigrated to the Colonies with her husband and three children. They were in Trade, he recalled. But wait. There was another Emily. He pounced upon it, turning it round in his head.

Certain now, he reached over and grasped her shoulder lightly to turn her towards him. "That's it! I remember who you are. You were Emily Merriweather, daughter of a shirttail heir to the Wilkensfield title." He snapped his thumb against his finger. "It was at Heatherwood Castle in Cornwall that we met."

Emily's eyes flashed. "So you *do* remember."

"Vaguely. You must have been about seven years old and I must have been about seventeen."

"I was nine. You had just turned sixteen. The party was in honour of your birthday, May 17."

He laughed. "So that was the year. Egad. You're incredible. You remember the precise date?"

"Believe me, Lord Berrington, the date is forever etched on my mind."

"Indeed? And why might that be?"

"You truly don't know, do you?"

"Know what? I recall that it was my sixteenth birthday when I received a carved leather saddle from my guardian. The Duke and Duchess of Heatherwood gave me an engraved silver comb and brush set." He grinned. "Ah, yes. The Russian emissary and his wife were there." He stroked his chin in deep thought. "Yes. I seem to remember they had a pretty little servant girl who spoke no English. Natasha was her name, I think."

Emily's voice held a note of malice. "I thought you might remember her. You acted like a moonling every time she came within shouting distance of you. Your tongue hung out so far that the servants were forced to bring you a dog collar and a leash."

James shook her playfully. "A bit of an exaggeration, wouldn't you say? Come now, Lady Emily. You're beginning to sound like a jealous harridan."

"Jealous! I was no such thing. I was angry. Yes, and I admit it. You embarrassed me in front of my friends, everyone."

"I embarrassed you? Don't be ridiculous. I hardly knew you."

"Please. Don't add insult to injury by pretending not to remember the occasion."

James, completely taken aback, didn't know whether to be amused or angry, but it was with some effort that he managed to keep a sober face. "On my honour, I vow that I do not remember any untoward incident, Lady Emily. If I did harm to you in any way, or in any way hurt your feelings, I am most heartily sorry."

"Your apology comes a little late. I'm not sure I can accept it after all these years."

"At least be charitable enough to enlighten me. My memory usually serves me well, but I cannot ima‒ ‒

the incident to which you refer. Did I spill food on your gown? Did I call you a name? Did I take away your toys?"

Emily glared. "Toys? I was nine years old. Do you think I still needed to be held on leading strings?"

"Then tell me, for God's sake, before I lose my wits."

Sorry now that she had started the whole thing, Emily darted her tongue across her lower lip. "You don't remember the game the twelve of us were playing in the garden that day?"

James slapped his forehead. "Lady Emily, have mercy! It was too many years ago. I scarcely remember being there, let alone what game we were playing."

"It was Prizes and Penalties. Your side was in the penalty box and you were up next for your team."

She waited, hoping he would remember without her having to go into detail, but his face was blank. She chewed her lip and would have turned away, but he held her there with his gaze.

"Go on," he demanded.

She cleared her throat. "Your side was in the penalty box. You were next in line."

"You already said that. Do continue. I'm all agog with curiosity."

Her eyes flashed. "The penalty you drew was to kiss a girl on the opposite team."

"Your team."

She nodded.

"Well... Go on. Did I perform my duty well?" He grinned and the smile lighted his face. "But wait. I remember now. I did play fair. I kissed the Russian chit square on the lips."

"Yes. And enjoyed every second of it." Emily saw his expression change from one of delight to one of puzzlement.

"I'm confused, Lady Emily. How did this serve to embarrass you? Had you never seen anyone kiss before?"

"But it was my turn!" she blurted out. "I was next in line. It was I you were supposed to kiss."

Lord Berrington's mouth spread from ear to ear as he sought unsuccessfully to contain his laughter. It took several minutes for him to regain control, minutes in which Emily felt the heat rise from the top of her bosom to her forehead. It required all of her willpower to keep from fanning herself with her kerchief.

"Laugh if you wish, my lord, but had you been in my place and suffered my shame and embarrassment at being skipped over for a servant, a foreigner at that, you wouldn't soon forgive and forget. I was teased without mercy for years after that."

"But it was only a game. We were just children."

"That does not signify. The insult was there and was not to be taken lightly."

He stuck out his lower lip. She could see that he had succeeded in containing his laughter, but a distinct twinkle remained in his eyes and she held her guard.

He put his hands on her shoulders and drew her still closer. "I remember it well, now that you refresh my memory. Alas, my dear lady, if only you had come to me for an explanation, I could easily have saved you such unbelievable distress."

"I sincerely doubt it," she murmured. "The act spoke for itself."

"Ah. But you've forgotten the name of the game."

She shook her head. "Prizes and Penalties. And you were in the penalty box."

He raised his eyes heavenwards. "Just so. And I suffered my penalty like a man. Had I but chosen you, Lady Emily, I would have been guilty of stealing the prize."

"Oh!" Emily drew a sharp breath, then let it out abruptly. "You are a double-tongued scoundrel, James Carstairs. Don't think you can charm me out of my anger. I was there, remember? I saw how bird-witted you looked when you kissed Natasha. You can't change the rules of the game. It was my turn, not hers."

Even as she said it, Emily realized how childish she sounded, but when he didn't laugh she hoped that he finally understood her feelings. She was afraid to look directly into his eyes. Instead, she concentrated on the curve of his mouth, edged by the faintly darkening shadow of a beard.

"Perhaps you are right, my lady. I see no solution to this dilemma except to beg your forgiveness." He lifted her chin in one hand and looked deep into her eyes as he spoke. "And take my penalty, which is so long overdue."

Before Emily could defend herself he bent and kissed her squarely on the mouth. As kisses went, it was far from offensive. His mouth was soft on hers, and he smelled sweetly of soap and some subtle fragrance she couldn't put a name to. He held her close in his arms for what seemed like an eternity. Common sense told her to fight back, but somehow she found herself holding on to him with no regard to propriety.

It was some time before he stopped to breathe. His mouth didn't stray far from her own; indeed, she felt first his warm breath on her cheek and then the soft brush of his lips on her forehead.

"S-stop this, my lord. You've no right to take advantage of me."

His mouth touched the base of her throat. "No right? Of course I have no right. I consider it an obligation."

She started to sputter, but he covered her mouth again and there was little she could do but allow him the liberty. Somewhere in the back of her mind, a small voice taunted her with the knowledge that she had never really tried to free herself and was, without doubt, thoroughly enjoying the strength of his embrace.

When he finally released her and held her at arm's length, Emily stiffened. "What do you mean, 'obligation'?"

His face reflected high good humour. "Madam, I have a reputation for paying my debts. If I cheated you when you were nine years old, then I am obliged to pay the penalty." His eyes gleamed. "With interest. It seems we have settled the first year's obligation. Shall we continue?"

"I... Certainly not!" She pushed him away and stepped back out of his reach. "Your behaviour, sir, is most ungentlemanly. Must I enlist the services of a chaperon to shield my good name?"

"Correct me if I am wrong, Lady Emily, but widowhood does allow women a certain measure of freedom, does it not? Even so, under the circumstances I hardly think you require a dragon to protect you."

"Does that mean in the future you will keep your distance?"

He looked shocked. "Lady Emily, if you think for one moment that I kissed you out of choice..." His voice trailed off.

She stared at him for several hard seconds before she turned abruptly and strode to the door. "I bid you good-night, sir." She was halfway up the stairs to the next floor when it suddenly occurred to her that he had made no promise at all. Even now she could sense that he was stroking his chin and smiling with that knowing look in his eyes. He had won again, and he knew it.

She heard him come to the foot of the stairs and call, "Where are you going, Lady Emily?"

"To my room to pack." The words were hardly out of her mouth when she realized she had brought nothing with her. She stopped short, looked down at him, and was about to qualify her words when he began to grin.

"The devil take you," she said. Turning quickly, she darted up the stairs with his laughter trailing behind her. It didn't make things easier to admit to herself that she was always running away from him.

THERE WAS NO DOUBT in Emily's mind that she and the countess would be back on the street the next day, and so it came as a surprise when the earl told her his plans the next morning at breakfast.

He buttered a scone, then laid it on the plate and took a sip of chocolate from a porcelain cup. "Are you all packed and ready to take your leave?" His face was innocence, right down to the smear of chocolate cream on his upper lip.

Emily gave him a scathing look. "You know very well I brought nothing with me."

"Good. That saves the maid having to unpack."

"I . . . I don't understand. We both know that the countess is a hoax. Why would you want us to stay on?"

Why, indeed? the earl asked himself. By keeping the women under his protection he was digging a pit without a bottom. One kiss had been sufficient to light fires in his blood which he had thought were forever cold to a woman's touch. A few hours alone with Lady Emily had been enough to make him start thinking of home and family and successors to the title he had inherited from his father.

He took another sip of chocolate, then cradled the cup in his hands. "If it will ease your mind a bit, Lady Emily, I am now convinced that you had no part in whatever devious sham this woman has concocted. I accept the fact that you were nothing more than an innocent pawn."

"How generous of you," Emily said dryly.

He shot her an impatient look. "The problem remains, however. What are we going to do with our little calico countess? And what is the motive behind her game of duplicity?"

"I suppose she could hope to get her hands on the jewels."

"Not likely. She isn't a complete dodderhead. Neither is she the product of the London slums which I mistook her for at first sight. I count her wise enough to know that it would take more than her word and a half dozen lucky coincidences before I would hand over the fortune in jewels which belonged to my mother." He leaned forward and rested his elbows on the table. "No, I can't let her go until we find out everything about her. This wasn't a moment's whim on her part. The woman is too well schooled in our family lore to have thought up the idea last week. We must find out what she wants and who, if anyone, is behind her."

"But that could take months."

The earl met Emily's gaze and held it with his own. "Yes. It could take a very long time."

"And you expect me to remain here with her?"

His eyes darkened. "Would you find that so distasteful?"

Emily put her hands on her lap to conceal their shaking. "You know very well that I am penniless. Nevertheless, I could not remain here simply as a guest. It would not be acceptable behaviour."

"Then you could be my official hostess. Attend to those things my housekeeper is too busy to do, arrange flowers, write invitations and thank-you notes, see to the refurbishing of the salon." His eyes sparkled as he continued, "If you are worried about the proprieties you have no need to fear. I could spread the word that a distant cousin has come to my aid, now that I have taken complete control of my estate. Your name is not completely forgotten, I trust, but Polite Society could easily have forgotten that we are related."

"You make it sound so easy. But how does the countess fit into all of this?"

"Save for her appetite for the grape and an untoward straightforwardness, she would not be out of place in London Society. We will continue to address her as Countess for the time being. For those who enquire, we shall merely say that she is visiting from the country, near Cornwall, and the two of you are companions to each other."

"And when she chucks you under the chin and calls you her son in a public gathering?"

The earl leaned back in his chair. "We'll let it be known that she is getting on in years and is often confused."

"I don't think we have a juggler's chance of getting away with this charade."

"Don't oppose me, Lady Emily. Between us we can get to the bottom of this unbelievable hoax and discover this woman's true identity. Of course we must take pains not to let her know that we see through her. Do you agree?"

Emily brought her elbows up to the table and leaned forward, making a steeple of her hands. "Do you have any idea what this entails? I have no money. The countess is penniless. If we are to move in polite circles we must dress the part."

"The cost is unimportant. I have more than enough money to last ten lifetimes. Say that you will help me."

"I shall think about it." She touched the tips of her fingers to her lips.

It was only then, when he saw the soft curve of her mouth and remembered the way her lips had felt against his when he kissed her last night, that James realized how desperately he wanted her to stay. "Do you want me to beg?" He laughed when he said it but only to cover the urgency in his voice.

Emily heard only the laughter. "All right. I agree to do it. But I fear we are building a house which may soon fall down around us."

"Then we'll build a stronger house."

"You have an answer for everything."

"So I've been told."

Emily looked at the clock. "Then tell me where the countess is. She should have been down to breakfast before this."

"Trust me. No one can keep up with the countess. I'll send a footman to look for her."

They found her in the conservatory some twenty minutes later.

"Oh, there you are, my dears. Come in, come in. I've been inspecting the beds and I must say, the hothouse is a disaster. How did you manage to neglect it so badly, my boy?"

James frowned. "It seemed a waste of time and money to maintain the conservatory. It was my, ah, mother's domain."

"I know. But that's no reason to let the beds lie fallow. We'll have to do something about them at once."

Emily studied the countess, who was dressed in a reasonably well-fitting morning gown of delicately flowered cotton. "We missed you at breakfast, Countess."

The woman waved her words aside. "I breakfasted in bed as always. Millie brought me a pot of chocolate and some scones. Fish is too heavy for me in the morning." She picked up a flowerpot and tapped it against the wooden bin until the dry ball of earth within was released. "I trust you weren't worried about me."

James watched her studiously. "In point of fact, we were."

"That's dear of you, my boy, but it is unnecessary now that I'm home. Everything will soon be as it was."

"We must talk about that. I have persuaded Lady Emily to remain with us for the present."

"*Lady Emily?*" The countess looked up sharply "What is this? Is there something you haven't told me?"

Emily folded her hands into the sleeves of her dress. "That is one of the things we need to talk about."

James offered his arm to the countess. "If you will accompany us to the library, perhaps we can find answers to all of your questions ... and mine."

"Oh James, I'm far too untidy. Let me refresh myself and I shall join you in an hour."

"If you prefer. I'll send Fredricks to show you the way to the library."

The countess smiled and patted his arm. "Dear James. You must consider me a complete chucklehead if you think I've forgotten the way to the library. It was my favourite room in the house."

"How could I have forgotten?" His voice was dry and it was with an expression of frustration and helplessness that he offered Emily his arm and escorted her into the hall.

"I know what notions you have in your head, Lady Emily, but we both realize that any number of people could have told the countess about the concealed wine cabinet. It was never meant to be kept secret." He tugged at the lapel of his waistcoat. "In the same vein, the impostor could have learned that my mother loved working with the plants in the conservatory."

"Yes, and I suppose they could have given her a floor plan of the house. So many coincidences. I wish I knew what to believe."

"One way or another we'll uncover the truth. The woman could hardly have invented this charade all on her own. Take my word for it, she is sure to trip herself into making a mistake if we but wait long enough."

TWO HOURS LATER, James was not quite so sure of himself. The countess took the news that Emily was, in fact, of noble birth with more delight than shock.

"I admit to suspecting the truth from the day we met. Quality is inbred, as much as the colour of one's hair and eyes." She patted Emily's hand. "It does make things easier, doesn't it? I am ever so grateful that you are titled. You may have looked the part of a menial, but you have much to learn about the way the lower classes behave.".

She turned to James without allowing either of them a chance to speak. "Isn't it nice, my boy—the three of us here together? It would have been a bit awkward to venture into Society if Emily had been unschooled in manners and polite behaviour. As it is, we shall have to begin at once to take our proper place among the haut ton."

James looked startled. "Oh, I say. This is moving far too fast." He looked to Emily for support.

She was tempted to let him stew in his own sauce but she thought better of it. "Lord Berrington, I believe you said something about paying a visit to the home of your former gardener."

"Yes, yes indeed. Hawkins Willoughby's his name. He may still be able to remember my mother and what she looked like."

The countess scoffed. "James, you are such a poor judge of people. Hawkins Willoughby was a dear man and an excellent gardener, but he was always a little hollow-headed when it came to what was going on about him." She pulled down one of a dozen books on flower cultivation and opened it with care. "Still, it would be good to see him again. Brighton is not so far distant."

James adjusted his neckcloth, which had apparently become too tight. "It hadn't occurred to me that you would be so eager to see him again, but yes, I think we should take care of the matter as soon as possible. Shall we say tomorrow?''

"Tomorrow? James, you have certainly become impetuous over the years. Couldn't you wait a week or so until we have our wardrobes in hand?''

"No. Tomorrow it is." He turned his back to the countess and spoke in a low voice to Emily. "I'll be hanged if I'll give her and her henchmen time to perpetrate another hoax." Then, speaking in a normal voice he said, "Lady Emily, will tomorrow be acceptable to you?''

"Yes, of course."

The countess spread her hands. "It's settled, then. We'll plan an early departure."

EARLY, FOR THE COUNTESS, apparently meant a few minutes short of the noon hour. James was already waiting in the carriage the next day when the two women were finally ready to leave. He opened the door and stepped down. His gaze immediately went to Emily, who was wearing a soft brown velvet gown, belted with an ebony satin sash.

The countess saw his close inspection and sniffed. "Yes, James, it's outdated to be sure, but Emily could hardly wear it in the Grecian style when it is two sizes too large for her. The belt was the only solution."

He assisted the countess aboard, then took Emily's hand. "I confess, Lady Emily, it was not the belt that caught my eye, but the slenderness of your waist."

Emily could not control her sudden blush, especially when the countess stuck her head out the door. "Don't be vulgar, James. I may be in my dotage but I do not allow such loose talk in the presence of ladies."

"My apologies to both of you," he said. Then, in a voice intended for Emily's ears alone, he muttered, "Sometimes she hears more than I think."

The two-and-one-half-hour drive to Brighton along the wide turnpike was accomplished rather pleasantly, except for one petulant remark from the countess, reprimanding James for rolling out the four-wheeled barouche with the driver seated high in front, instead of the state carriage. He gave her a droll look and inquired as to her comfort or lack of it.

Her expression was equally quelling. "It is hardly a question of comfort, James. It's appearances which count."

Emily made haste to turn the conversation in the direction of the number of vehicles on the road, and James, grateful for the reprieve, remarked that a country fair was being held at a nearby town.

Hawkins Willoughby had retired to a small but comfortable rural cottage outside Brighton. His rheumy eyes studied them for a brief moment when he opened the newly whitewashed Dutch doors.

James, standing first, spoke to him. "Willoughby, my good man. I trust we're not intruding. I've brought some company with me this time."

"Aye and 'tis you, Lord Berrington. Come in, come in. 'Tis good to see you it is, milord."

Emily noticed that despite his stooped shoulders and face which was furrowed as deeply as newly turned soil, Hawkins Willoughby was quite presentable in his own way. His frosty hair was well trimmed and remarkably thick for a man of such advanced years.

James ignored the awkward moment when introductions should have taken place by making a fuss over finding chairs for the women in the sparsely furnished room. He seated the countess in a woven-reed rocking-chair, then ushered Emily to a straight-backed chair he pulled from beside a pine work-table. Willoughby seated himself on a hand-hewn wooden bench by the fireplace and James came to stand behind the countess.

He managed to get through the next few minutes by making small talk about Willoughby's retirement, the gardens and the weather, but finally James drew a deliberate breath and laughed. "Willoughby, my good man, I've been waiting to see if you recognized my friend here." He put his hand obligingly on the countess's shoulder. "She remembers you from the old days when you kept the gardens at the estate."

Willoughby squinted. "Is that so? It's been a parcel of years, milord, but I could never forget the gardens. Roses, we had, and apple trees heavy with fruit."

James grinned, feeling more sure of himself than ever. "But surely you couldn't forget this lovely woman. You knew her so well."

"Aye. I never forgets a face, milord. Some things ain't so clear as they once was, but faces... I knows faces like I knows me own."

James shot a triumphant look at Emily and his voice grew strong with conviction. "Are you saying, my good man, that you don't remember the lady's face?"

"No, milord. I didn't say that."

James strode across the room and back. "Then speak up, man. Either you remember her face or you don't."

"No need to get riled up, sir, beggin' your pardon. I don't remember or disremember the lady's face, because the truth is I can't *see* her face." He chuckled. "You couldn't guess, could you? I've been blind now for near on two years."

CHAPTER SIX

"BLIND!" All three visitors spoke the word with varying degrees of surprise.

Hawkins Willoughby drew a pipe from his coat, tamped it with his forefinger, then clamped it between his teeth. Easing himself round on the bench, he reached unerringly into an earthen mug and extracted a straw. While they watched, he leaned towards the fireplace, ignited the end of the straw, and applied it to the bowl of his pipe. He sucked noisily for a few seconds, then threw the wasted straw into the fireplace.

"Aye, blind," he said.

James sounded genuinely sympathetic when he spoke. "I'm most dreadfully sorry, Willoughby. I had no idea. Is there nothing to be done?"

"Nothing, milord, 'lessen you can give me back me youth. 'Tis naught but old age what took me sight. It came on slow-like so I had some time to get used to it. That and the pension you gives me makes it tolerable to live with." He drew deeply on the pipe and expelled the smoke into the room before placing the pipe on the stone apron which fronted the fireplace.

"But tell me, Lord Berrington, sir. Who is this lady what remembers me? And the other? She wears lavender, I think."

Emily smiled. "How uncanny. You are right, Mr. Willoughby. I am very partial to the scent of lavender.

My name is Emily Harding, Lady Wallingford. I am a guest at Berrington House."

Willoughby acknowledged the introduction with a bob of his head, then turned towards where the countess was seated. She would have spoken but James interrupted. "It is about this other lady that we have come here, Willoughby." James leaned against the mantel and began the story of how the countess had claimed that she was his long-lost mother.

"And so you see, Willoughby," he concluded, "although there is no doubt in my mind that she is an impostor, I want to prove once and for all that I am right. Unfortunately, there is no one left, except for a relative or two in America, who can remember what my mother looked like. It has, after all, been seventeen years."

The countess finally broke her silence. "Hawkins Willoughby, you old coot. You don't need your eyes to tell you I'm no modeller. And you're no clodpate just because you're a bit long in the tooth." She leaned closer. "Remember the herb garden I made you plant under the oak tree?"

"Aye, milady. And it never took. I told you there was too much shade."

"And the honeysuckle we planted around the gazebo?"

"Drew the bees, it did. You used to take tea there until they buzzed round your ears and you made me tear it out and plant—"

"Roses," the countess interrupted.

"Aye. Roses and lilies what bloomed on St. Swithin's Day."

James slapped his gloves against his thigh. "Enough. Think about it, my good man," he said to Willoughby. "You are treating this impostor as if she were indeed my mother. We all know this couldn't possibly be. My mother and father are buried in the graveyard at St. Nicholas's Church.''

"Aye, sir. And that's God's truth. I remember the day they dug the graves. Made a fine mess them lads did, tearin' up the roots of the cedars what grow along the side o' the graveyard.''

Emily clasped her hands together and leaned towards him. "Then you were there the day they were buried. You saw with your own eyes that they were placed in the graves.''

"And a sad day it was, too. His lordship sufferin' so, and him not much more than a babe himself.''

"Oh, come now, Willoughby. I was eleven years old. I haven't forgotten the day.''

"Nor should ye. My lord and lady worshipped the ground you walked on.''

James strode across the room. His voice sounded as stiff as his back and the set of his mouth. "I cherish their memory, Mr. Willoughby, and that is why I cannot countenance anyone who would presume to usurp my mother's name.''

Willoughby muttered something unintelligible, then picked up his pipe and clamped it between his teeth. James looked first at Emily, who appeared deeply unnerved. Then his gaze was drawn to the countess. Oddly, she seemed to be totally unshaken by the corroboration of her burial.

Devil take the woman, James thought. *She must have nerves of granite.* What must he do, he wondered, to break her and uncover those who were working with her?

The countess rose from her chair and walked over to where the old gardener sat on his bench. "It's all right,

Hawkins. I understand," she said, patting him on the shoulder. "Neither of us is as young as we used to be. Isn't it strange how things seem to escape us as the years multiply? I had completely forgotten until this moment about the summer you planted grass along the south terrace."

"Mayhap you didn't want to remember, milady. Seein' as how you wanted clover planted there. But 'tis right you are. Me head plays tricks on me when I try to bethink the way it used to be when I worked for you and his lordship."

James had had enough. The countess had hit the mark. Old Willoughby was without doubt confused. One moment he remembered seeing the real countess buried, and in the next breath he seemed to address the impostor as if she were the countess reincarnated.

James motioned to Emily. "Come, Lady Emily. We mustn't overstay our welcome. Willoughby, thank you for speaking to us. I trust that you will stay well until we see you again."

Willoughby rose and bowed stiffly. "It pleasured me to see you again, milord...and miladies. May you have a safe journey back to London."

The countess patted his shoulder in a kindly way. "The gardens are not the same without you, Hawkins. No one keeps the flower beds so bright nor the walkways swept so clean."

He bowed deeply in her general direction, thanked her, and ushered them to the door. They were just getting into the carriage when he came rushing outside. "Your lordship. Beggin' your pardon, sir, I just remembered."

James turned from helping the countess into the carriage. "Yes, Willoughby, what is it?"

"I know how it was then. You were but a wee lad and we didn't want to hurt you."

Emily felt the hair rise on the back of her neck. She stood beside James, close enough that she could see the muscles tense at the side of his jaw. His voice rasped slightly when he spoke. "You have remembered something else, then?"

"Aye, sir. Indeed I have. And I recall thinkin' at the time that maybe we was doin' the wrong thing."

James's hand tightened on the carriage door until his knuckles shone white. Emily knew that he was using all his self-control not to shake the man, who seemed determined to prolong the agony. But when James spoke his voice had softened. "If there is anything, anything else you can tell me, Mr. Willoughby, I will be grateful to hear it."

"It's about them graves, sir. 'Tis true, there was two headstones. You saw them yourself. Pink granite they was—one for your papa and one for your mama. Sittin' right next to each other there 'neath the cedar tree. The one with the top what was struck by lightnin'."

"Yes. I remember them. The graves were placed near a statue of a winged angel."

"Not graves, sir, beggin' yer pardon. There was only one grave—your papa's. Her ladyship's body was niver found. They gave her a headstone and said a few words over her grave to make it easier for you to understand that she was gone."

It was several minutes before anyone spoke. Emily, seeing that all the colour had drained from James's face, reached up to grasp his arm, but he appeared not to notice.

When he spoke the words sounded harsh around the edges, as if they were hewn from rough wood. "Do you mean that my mother's body was never found?"

Willoughby shifted uneasily, as if unable to grasp the possible consequences of how he might answer. He visibly shrank into himself.

"She *was* gone, you know, sir, your mother. They was all gone. Seventy-two souls, with captain and crew. Every blessed one o' them went to the bottom."

There was a brief, intense silence and then the countess leaned out of the carriage window and laid her hand on James's arm. A gentle smile lighted her face. "Not everyone perished, my dear. There was one who was saved. And I've come home."

What followed could only be described as a state of numbed confusion. Poor old Hawkins Willoughby kept testing the air with his nose and tapping the ground with his cane as if trying to regain a sense of reality. James withdrew into himself, speaking only twice, once to order the driver to take them back to London post-haste, and once flatly to refuse the countess's suggestion that they delay long enough to stop at St. Nicholas's Church to visit the graveyard.

As for Emily, she was all but lost in a state of wonder. Nothing could have convinced her that events would unfold in such a bizarre manner. The unbelievable now seemed all but indisputable. This woman could, after all, prove to be the real Countess of Berrington. Indeed, there was little left to lend doubt to her claim.

Emily stole a sidelong glance at James, who sat slouched in his seat, his chin buried deep in the collar of his greatcoat, his eyes glazed and unfocused. His mouth

was set in a hard line which boded ill for anyone who
thought to disturb him.

Only the countess seemed at peace with herself. She
hummed a disjointed sort of melody as she surveyed the
passing landscape. Her hands rested quietly in her lap
or snuggled together inside the velvet muff she had res-
urrected from the depths of a cedar chest that very
morning—a morning which seemed a lifetime ago.
Emily would have given a day of her life to know what
was going through the woman's mind. After an hour
passed the countess finally closed her eyes and drifted
off to sleep.

Emily was relieved. She dreaded facing a prolonged
discussion of what had transpired. Too much might be
said that could never be taken back. They needed time
to sort out their thoughts, weigh all the questions and
answers before committing themselves one way or the
other. From the look on James's face, he was in no
condition at the moment to talk to anyone.

She willed him to look at her, but it was only when
the carriage hit a pothole that his gaze met hers for an
instant, then darted away. In that brief contact Emily
saw a mixture of emotions which was both angry and
confused. James hadn't given in. She was sure of it. But
his doubt was beginning to show through his determination not to believe the countess.

WHEN THEY FINALLY arrived back at Berrington House,
James, stiff-lipped and tense, said he would see them in
the library within the hour.

Once she had freshened herself, Emily spent the in-
terim pacing the floor and looking at the clock. The
countess, seemingly relaxed and happy, summoned

Millie to assist with renovations on her wardrobe. The hour dragged into an eternity.

James was standing by his desk when they went downstairs. He bowed stiffly, then motioned them to be seated.

"I'll make this as brief as possible. I know this has been a most trying day." He cleared his throat. "Taking into consideration the information old Willoughby has given us, I have determined, for the time being at least, to continue with things as they are." He turned to the countess. "That does not mean I accept your claim as genuine. It only means that it bears a certain degree of consideration."

The countess opened her fan and passed it slowly in front of her face. She appeared to study James for a moment across its scalloped lace edge, then snapped it shut and secured it against the ivory handle.

"You are well within your rights, James, to question this miracle which saved me from the jaws of death, but the time has come for you to accept the truth." She untied the ribbon from her wrist and dropped the fan onto the table in a gesture of irritation. "I am not young. There is much to be done before I take my place beside your father in the graveyard at St. Nicholas's Church. For one thing, I wish to see you marry and produce an heir to carry on our family name. Your wife must have a place provided for her in the ranks of Society. It is my responsibility to see that she is so honoured."

James looked over at Emily, who tried without success to mask her surprise. The countess was determined to waste no time. What she lacked in diplomacy she made up for in pure gall. But admittedly, she had a certain charm about her which was intriguing.

She continued as if unaware of the undercurrents swirling about the room. "We must lose no time in putting our wardrobes together and sending out calling-cards. I think it would be best if we gave a soirée. Don't you agree, Emily?"

"Well, I—"

James cut in quickly. "No. That is, I think it would be too obvious. As it is, I will be entertaining some members of Parliament and their ladies in the near future. That occasion should be sufficient, I should think, to introduce you to the ton."

The countess sniffed. "Adequate, perhaps, but hardly the sort of thing I had in mind." She stood and went to the table next to the window. "Would someone care for a brandy? There is a decided chill in the room."

They both knew she wasn't speaking of the temperature. The fire which was always kept burning in the grate was more than enough to heat the room.

The brandy did its work, and within a short time the countess was snoring. Emily did her best to keep the conversation from falling apart completely, but James contributed very little. When Emily finally lost patience she confronted him. "You are still convinced that she is not your mother. I can see it in your eyes. But what do you propose to do now?"

"What do you suggest?"

"I . . . I don't know. If it were I in such a strange circumstance, I think I would accept her for what she claims to be."

He raised his head and stared at Emily. "Do you have any idea what that entails? Along with the title of Dowager Countess, go a great many responsibilities, not to mention a magnitude of power and wealth. It will be hers until I marry and she relinquishes the power to my wife."

Emily spread her hands in a gesture of finality. "Then I suppose the solution to your problem is to marry."

He frowned. "The absurdity of the suggestion is only equalled by the ridiculous situation."

"Then it is your intention to allow the title to die with you?"

"I didn't say that. Of course I intend to marry. When I find the woman I want I shall wed and produce an heir."

Emily laughed. "And the woman has no choice in the matter. She will simply fall at your feet in perfect obedience and humility."

James aimed a dark look directly at Emily's face. "Don't twist my words. You know what I mean."

"What you mean is that you must be convinced that no woman is good enough to be your wife. Otherwise you would have married by now, or at least have been betrothed." She smiled when she spoke, but at the same time she suspected there was an element of truth to her words. "You aren't exactly a moonling or a garlickeater. I fancy the mothers of eligible daughters must flock about you like vultures on a battleground."

"Your *fancy* will get you into trouble one day, Lady Emily. In truth, although I have attended social functions, I have had little time to canary around, what with all my father's affairs, which had been neglected while I was going to school." He pulled a bell cord to summon the butler. "And speaking of duties, I expect to be away for a few days. My staff will be at your service while I am gone. If you wish to begin preparations for the party on the twenty-fifth, you'll find a sheet of instructions and a list of names for the invitations here in the desk.''

Emily nodded, then pressed her hands together. "Is there somewhere I can reach you if you are needed?"

"That won't be necessary. My butler can take care of whatever problem might arise."

Fredricks entered at that moment and James asked him to have someone see the countess to her rooms.

Emily found it hard to deal with this cold, emotionless side to James's nature. She wanted to break through his shell of reserve, but he gave her no opportunity. A few minutes later he suggested that she, too, repair to her room and allow him to attend to last-minute details before his impending departure.

She dropped a slow curtsy, never once removing her gaze from his face, and left the room.

It was several hours later, as she lay awake watching the progress of the moon across a cloudless sky, that she heard his carriage rattle down the drive and into the cobblestone street.

THE HOUSE WAS NOT THE SAME after James left. The servants behaved with scrupulous courtesy. Everyone from Fredricks down to the least of the scullery maids treated Emily with as much respect as if she were the mistress of the house, rather than a temporary guest of the establishment. In truth, it should have been the countess who held the reins, but it was obvious that at least part of the time she was short a few spokes of the carriage wheel. This happened most frequently when she had been pinching the sherry. Unfortunately, the sherry was in abundant supply.

Emily decided that the only way to distract the countess from the grape was to cater to her interest in fashion. James had given Emily permission to charge whatever they needed to his accounts, as well as to use whatever gowns they could find stored in the attic since it was his intention to dispose of them. Emily was shocked. There was a fortune in fine silks, velvets, satins, and brocades. Of course the styles were dated and the fit was off, but between the two of them and with the help of a seamstress they should be able to create wardrobes for less than half the price of custom-made gowns.

The countess was exuberant. "Think style, my dear, not fashion. It's the true French way. Fashions live for the moment but style is eternal. We can begin with the patterns. The seamstress, with my help, of course, can take a simple pattern and create a multitude of designs."

Emily watched her with curiosity. "Then you can cut patterns as well as sew? Where did you learn how to do that?"

"Well I . . . well, isn't that strange? I can't seem to recall exactly where. I know that I decorated hats and worked occasionally as a seamstress to buy food and lodging after the shipwreck. But as to precisely where I learned the skill, I couldn't say. Strange, isn't it, how little things escape from memory as we mature?"

"Um, I suppose so."

It occurred to Emily later that although dates and names of people and places seemed to be beyond Lady Marguerite's grasp, her fingers had lost little of their nimbleness. Emily, the countess, and Millie worked for hours on end to put together the beginning of wardrobes suitably elegant for their entrance into Society.

When Emily found it necessary to devote her energies to planning the party James had set for the night of the twenty-fifth, they enlisted the services of Yvette, the upstairs maid whom Emily had encountered in the ballroom that first day. She was adept with the needle, had an eye for style, and her sweet singing voice cheered the women while they worked. Emily had Fredricks bring the desk into the sewing room so that she could share in the camaraderie while addressing invitations.

It was only when she was alone that her thoughts turned to James and how much she missed him.

HE RETURNED A WEEK LATER.

Emily was in the conservatory gathering flowers for the large urn in the entrance hall when Fredricks opened the French doors and came in. "Pardon, your ladyship. Shall we serve dinner in the dining room tonight?"

"Oh, I think not, Fredricks. Lady Marguerite and I prefer to use the small table in the library when we are alone."

"His lordship has returned, ma'am. He instructed me to say that he would be joining you for sherry before dinner."

Emily struggled to keep her voice calm. "Very well, Fredricks. Under the circumstances you may serve dinner in the dining room." She held the bouquet of orange blossoms and pale pink primroses to her face and inhaled their fragrance. "You might use the pink linen cloth tonight, and the gold candelabra."

Fredricks allowed himself only the briefest quiver of an eyebrow before he acknowledged the order and bowed. After he was gone Emily laid her cutting shears on the bench with unnecessary violence.

Now why did I say that? she thought. *Everyone knows the gold candelabra and the pink linen cloth are reserved for festive occasions. James is going to think I made too much of his first dinner at home.* She was tempted to run below stairs to rescind the order but that would only serve to call more attention to it. Besides, she mused, holding the flowers against her shawl and smiling a secret smile, the pink linen cloth would blend beautifully with her new burgundy-and-rose gown. Oh, it was lovely having something new to wear, even if the fabric itself was nearly twenty years old.

She took extra care with her toilette that evening. Yvette had asked permission to comb Emily's hair and although Millie at first took affront, she had to admit that she was glad to be relieved of the task for which she was ill-equipped.

"Now then, madam," Yvette said, holding the mirror so that Emily could see the back of her head. "Does it not please you? The little curls, the smooth upsweep, and the wee tuck at the back of your head? Wait! I have just the thing. I found a decorated comb in the panniers of one of the gowns we were working on today." She opened a sandalwood box and took out the comb. It sparkled with insets of violet and clear glass.

"No...I couldn't."

"But you must. It is the final touch." She brushed her fingertips against her lips and blew a kiss.

Emily laughed. "I admit, it does look enchanting. All right. I'll wear it just this once." She turned around to face the mirror. "Is the countess ready to go downstairs?"

"*Oui.* She asked me to say that she would meet you in the library."

"Oh, dear. I hope she isn't taking nips of the sherry."

"I think she wanted to speak to her son."

"I see," Emily said. So the servants had already accepted that the countess was indeed the genuine article. She sighed. The question was, when would James come to believe what the evidence so clearly supported? And if he did, where would it leave her? She would find it difficult to return to a life of poverty. Even worse was her fear of being caught by Mr. Grimstead and sent to debtor's prison.

But she couldn't allow herself to think about it now. She was safe for the time being. James was home. And he was waiting to see her in the library. Safe? She remembered suddenly how it had felt when he held her in his arms and kissed her. She was hardly safe. She was a victim of her own weaknesses, and that could prove to be the most dangerous position of all.

Emily took one last look in the mirror, thanked Yvette for her services, and went downstairs. Fredricks opened the door to the library and announced her in his deep baritone voice.

James, standing by the window, turned and looked at her. He was too stunned to greet her properly. What had happened to Lady Emily could only be considered a transformation. Was it her hair, shining so soft and gold-brown in the lamplight? Was it the way the pink brocade gown clung to her soft curves and whispered seductively as she walked? Or was it because her eyes and mouth tilted upwards so bewitchingly when she came towards him? He cursed halfheartedly to himself. He was completely bewitched by her. Hardly an hour had passed in the entire week when she wasn't uppermost in his thoughts, but he must not allow himself to lose control.

He bowed deeply. "Good evening, Lady Emily. You look exceedingly well tonight."

Emily was nonplussed. Did he expect her to look unwell? Or was it simply a reluctant compliment? She dropped an equally elaborate curtsy. "May I return the compliment, sir. I trust that you had a successful journey and that your health has not suffered."

James flushed. If truth be told, he felt much better just being able to see her, even if it did mean coming to sword's point more often than not. He offered her a glass of sherry.

"Suffice it to say I missed the comforts of home. Fredricks tells me you have taken command of the staff like a general in charge of a regiment." He saw the look of alarm on Emily's face and hastened to reassure her. "I grant you, Lady Emily, he meant it as an accolade. The house has never looked better, nor have the servants ever seemed more content."

"Thank you. I hope I have not overstepped my bounds."

"Most certainly not. Mrs. Grover has nothing but praise for the way you have lifted the burdens from her shoulders."

They turned as the countess, who had been browsing through a book on the cultivation of ground creepers, came towards them and extended both hands.

"My dears. Isn't this charming? Here we are together again. Doesn't Emily look lovely, James?"

He turned his gaze once again to Emily but this time he saw only her eyes. He felt himself drawn to her like a man in search of a sultan's treasure. He was hypnotized by her wit and beauty and—yes, the air of secrecy she tried so hard to conceal. The more she hid it, the more he was determined to unearth her secret. But it wasn't easy, confound it. His trip to her home village had served only to unearth events leading up to a year ago, events which she had already revealed to him. But there had to be more.

The countess broke the spell with a playful poke in his ribs. "James, are you bedazzled? Tell Emily how adorable she looks."

James inclined his head. "Adorable, yes. May I say that your taste is exquisite in the gowns you ladies have chosen. Did you favour Miss Cadwalader's shop in Beacon Street?"

The countess chuckled. "Don't you remember this gown, James? I wore it at Montagu House in Portman Square the day Mrs. Montagu gave her breakfast for seven hundred people to open her room of feathers. No, of course you wouldn't remember. You were but three or four years old, if I recall correctly."

James gave her a dry look. "The gown is lovely still. And it pleases me to see that this one has been shortened sufficiently so that you are not likely to stumble."

Emily's hand flew to her mouth, as if to silence him, but it was already too late. The countess laughed. "Dear boy. You're referring to the blue-and-silver brocade. I admit it was something of a fiasco when my hem fell down and nearly tripped me up. I thought I had lost more weight than I imagined, but my memory finally served me well. Remember the season that your Aunt Harriet spent with us while the Major was in Africa?"

James shook his head and started to say something, but the countess went into a long-winded explanation of the events leading up to the season of the Mandeville come-out. There was no interrupting her. Emily gave James an I-tried-to-warn-you look, but all he could do was stand by and try to appear interested.

"And so you see—" the countess tilted her head back and looked him in the eye "—your Aunt Harriet and I decided to dress alike for the party at the palace. It made quite a sensation—never mind that she was seven inches taller than I was. We were quite the hit of the Season despite the fact that we were both married and long past our come-outs.''

She apparently saw the glazed look on his face. ''Really, James, don't be so moon-witted. Don't you see what I'm saying? When I took the blue brocade from the armoire and decided to wear it that night when we first arrived, I pulled out the wrong dress. It was Harriet's dress. My own identical dress must still be packed away in some trunk up in the attic.''

James looked sceptical. And who could blame him? Emily thought. Marguerite's explanation was logical— and yet so utterly convenient. Added to that, enough time had passed for her to have manufactured a plausible excuse.

Emily put her hand on the countess's arm. ''I wonder, Countess, if you wouldn't like to sit down near the fire?''

''No, my dear, I think I'll have another sip of sherry before Fredricks announces dinner.''

James frowned and Emily hastened to intervene. ''You wouldn't want to spoil your appetite. Cook is preparing roast pheasant and rice.'' She took the older woman's arm and steered her away from the sherry decanter.

As she turned, James noticed the comb Emily was wearing in the back of her hair. He set down his glass on the table with undue force and followed Emily across the room.

He put his hands firmly on her shoulders and turned her round. ''When the cat's away the mice will play. Isn't that right, Lady Emily?''

"I . . . I beg your pardon? What is it?"

"This!" he said, reaching around her and plucking the comb from her hair. His face was livid. "Tell me, Lady Emily. Just how did you manage to gain access to the family vaults?"

CHAPTER SEVEN

IT DIDN'T TAKE a soothsayer to tell Emily that James was furious. She wasn't sure whether to laugh or cry. Her first impulse was to strike out at him, but she could hardly do that. Especially when he looked so stricken. She slowly pulled her shawl round her and raised her gaze to meet his.

"If you are implying that I stole the comb, my lord, you disappoint me. In truth, Yvette found the comb in the panniers of one of the gowns we were reconstructing. Since it appeared to be of small value, I decided to wear it tonight to complement my gown."

"Of small value? The stones are diamonds and amethysts. It was a gift to my mother from Princess Isolde."

The countess reached for it. "Oh, I had forgotten about this. Yes," she said, holding the comb up to the light, "it's true. They are gems, but of an inferior quality. Not surprising, though," she mused. "The Spanish princess was famous for bestowing gifts of little consequence on anyone and everyone. Perhaps that is why we failed to contain it in the vault. Keep it, Emily. It's yours."

She handed it over to Emily, who immediately gave it to James. Emily's voice was tight with anger. "Thank you, but I couldn't accept it."

The countess shook her head and placed her hand over her heart. "Don't be ridiculous, my dear. It's but a trifle. The stones are mere chips."

"It is not the value that concerns me."

"Then what?"

Before Emily could frame the words to express her hurt at James's lack of trust, Fredricks appeared to announce that dinner was served. Without another word, Emily walked stiffly from the room and down the corridor towards the dining room.

Dinner was a disaster. The service was excellent, the decor and the food divine, but the conversation, or lack of it, was confined to reminiscences from the countess or her guarded questions to James, who responded with equally guarded answers concerning his whereabouts for the past week. When the meal was finally over and the countess had excused herself on the grounds of fatigue, Emily made her own excuses.

James detained her at the door. "I must apologize, Lady Emily. I accused you before I had a chance to think. I consider my words not only unfounded but appallingly churlish. Will you forgive me?"

He was standing with his hand braced on the doorframe above her head so that she was captured, if not imprisoned, by his arm. Although there was no actual physical contact, she felt compelled to remain there.

His apparent sincerity surprised her. "I . . . I suppose I can understand your concern, my lord, your mistrust of me. But I hasten to assure you that I have no desire to steal from you, or anyone else."

"I know that. It is only—"

"What?"

"It is only that there is so much about you that you haven't told me."

"I see no need, no justifiable reason to bare my soul to you. Or for you to confide in me, for that matter."

He cocked an eyebrow. "I wasn't aware that I had been less than candid with you."

"Oh, indeed! You were certainly less than straight-forward concerning your absence during this past week."

A muscle twitched at the side of his temple. So, she had missed him and was curious about where he had gone. Had she questioned Fredricks? No. She wouldn't. She had too much pride to stoop to quizzing the servants. He was tempted to tease her, but then he saw how ill at ease she was and he straightened.

"If you wished to know where I was, Lady Emily, all you had to do was ask."

He waited, but she remained silent. *Stubborn woman.* She was as good at games as he was. Maybe better, considering that once again she had avoided any personal revelations. The thought sobered him, but at the same time it sent a thrill of excitement singing through his blood. He stroked his chin.

"Now that the countess has made herself quite presentable, would the two of you care to join me for a stroll in the Park tomorrow?"

"I . . . I'm sure the countess would be delighted."

"The countess, eh? And you?"

"I would consider it a pleasant change. What time do you wish us to be ready?"

"I believe four o'clock is the fashionable hour. The ladies of the ton will be about. It should make an excellent, if informal, occasion for your first appearance, it seems to me."

"Thank you. I will inform the countess." She dropped a curtsy and started to walk away. At the last minute she turned to see him still watching her. "May I say in all honesty, Lord Berrington, it is very nice to have you home again."

He bowed. "Thank you, Lady Emily. Suffice it to say that the week I spent in Cornwall seemed more like a month in its duration."

She stood still for a moment, allowing the information to sink in. Cornwall? Why had he gone back to her home? Was it merely a coincidence, or had he gone there to ask questions about her background? She saw that it was not his intention to embellish his surprising statement and she was not about to pursue it. Instead, she inclined her head briefly and bade him good-night.

When Emily looked into the bedroom adjoining hers, the countess was getting ready to retire. She invited Emily to sit on the bench at the foot of the bed, then paused in the midst of brushing her hair.

"What is it, my dear? What's happened? I can see you are near to bursting with excitement."

Emily pressed her hands together in front of her bosom. "His lordship has invited us to stroll with him tomorrow afternoon in Hyde Park."

The countess dropped the brush on the floor and stood up. "Dear heaven. It's begun. Emily, my love, we are about to be announced to London Society. Do you have any idea what this means?"

"I suspect the first thing it means is that we must do something about our bonnets. We won't have time to go to the hatmakers."

The countess waved Emily's comments aside. "Never fear, my dear. We shall manage. There are dozens of hats and bonnets in the armoire in the attic. We shall work wonders with them."

It occurred to Emily the next day that the true wonder was the energy with which the countess undertook the task of planning their wardrobe for the outing. The old woman selected a silver-grey velvet gown piped at the hem with narrow bands of red and black. The design was repeated in a short pelisse which fell in soft folds from the wide collar to just below her fingertips.

Emily chose a walking dress of French-blue linen accented with a Belgian lace fichu and cuffs of the same ivory lace design. She had altered the dress to the latest style by raising the waistline to fall straight to the hem from just below the bosom. Unlike the countess, who easily took a chill, Emily decided to forgo the cape.

But it was the hats which tilted the scale. The countess cornered Yvette and another maid, Penelope, just after the clock struck nine. Within the hour they were drowning in piles of veiling net, feathers, silk, straw, and artificial flowers. Emily joined them a short time later and discovered with some surprise that she, too, had an innate sense of style and design.

Penelope had a tendency to overembellish with flowers and feathers, but a word of caution from the countess kept her in line. By the time the clock struck the hour of three, the women had created two bonnets and made over two hats into stylish chapeaux.

The countess tucked her hair under a fetching straw bonnet which curved about her head in an oval and tied beneath her chin. "Correct me if I am wrong, Lady Emily, but don't you agree, we shall be the envy of the ton?"

"I confess, I had no idea we could do so well. Of course much of the credit goes to the fine quality of the hats we used to make over into the new designs."

Yvette held up a confection of blue silk forget-me-nots and green silk net affixed to a white straw bonnet. "*Mon Dieu!* Even in Paris one could not find such a lovely chapeau. *C'est ravissant!*"

The countess was more sober. "Well, we shall see, shan't we, when we take our stroll in Hyde Park? Suffice it to say that our appearance can either be to our advantage or disadvantage."

Emily detected the note of uneasiness in her voice and worried that perhaps the countess was undertaking too much at once. She was, after all, not a young woman. But when Emily suggested they put off the outing to another day, the countess was appalled.

"Nonsense, my dear girl. I've waited nearly seventeen years to take back my rightful place in Society. I'll not delay an hour longer than necessary. Penelope, be a good girl and run along and ask Millie to draw my bath. We have scarce enough time to get ready. Dear heaven," she murmured, casting a wary glance towards the window, "don't let it rain."

THE WEATHER SEEMED to be on the side of the countess. By the time the carriage had deposited them near the entrance to the Park, the afternoon sun, thanks to a freshening breeze from the sea, had temporarily cleared the air of smoke. Already the barouches, phaetons, and gigs were lined up in the waiting area while their owners strolled the crowded walks along the Serpentine or stopped to view the fountains and flower gardens.

James offered an arm to both Lady Marguerite and Emily as they entered the flow of well-dressed pedestrians. Emily thought he looked even more handsome than usual in his fawn-coloured breeches, ivory cravat, and beaver. He intercepted her gaze. "May I say that I am blessed with two of the most attractive ladies in the Park? It seems we are creating a bit of a janty."

The countess nodded regally to a young couple who had the audacity to stare with more boldness than good manners. She partially covered her mouth with her hand. "Smile, James. They expect it of us. It is part of the price we must pay for our noble blood."

He shot a look at Emily, who tried hard to control her laughter. Before he could say anything, they were detained by a woman and her three young daughters, two of whom were of marriageable age. The woman all but ignored Emily and the countess as she fixed her eye on James.

He separated himself from Emily and the countess and bowed. "Mrs. Castorbridge, young ladies, how nice to see you," James said, and would have walked on, but the matron put her hand upon his arm.

"Lord Berrington, how lovely to see you on the promenade. Do stop long enough to chat and... introduce us to your friends," she added with seeming reluctance.

James inhaled deeply. "But of course. Mrs. Castorbridge, Miss Bertha, Miss Agatha, and Miss Drucilla. May I present Lady Marguerite and Lady Wallingford." He saw that the woman was waiting for more. He frowned and cleared his throat. "The ladies are residing at Berrington House for the present."

"Oh, indeed? Distant relatives, are they?"

James muttered something unintelligible, but Mrs. Castorbridge took it as an affirmative. She preened her hair, which was an odd shade of pinkish red, as if the henna had curdled in the sun.

"Can you imagine! Silly me. I thought perhaps you had finally bitten the thread and taken a wife." She laughed and patted her eldest daughter's shoulder. "My Miss Bertha will be happy to know that she still has a chance to capture your roguish heart, Lord Berrington."

Miss Bertha smiled up at him with large, cowlike eyes and bobbed a curtsy. James gave a curt nod and adjusted his cravat. It was several more minutes before they were able to escape the Castorbridge clutches, but not before an invitation was pressed upon them to come to tea on the following Thursday. The countess declined with what Emily suspected was an admirable show of restraint.

When they were safely out of earshot, Emily looked around James at the countess, who walked stiffly erect. "Lady Marguerite, you were barely civil to that poor woman. I thought you would jump at the chance to accept her invitation to tea."

"Why ever would I do that? She is a nobody. A desperate mother with an eye towards palming off one of her daughters on the first eligible man without webbed feet and pointed ears." The countess sniffed delicately into a lace handkerchief. "An opportunist if I ever saw one."

James raised an eyebrow and whispered to Emily out of the side of his mouth. "She should well know about that."

Emily frowned. "Careful. Your mother hears more than you might think."

James bit off a tart reply when three women who had signalled him approached from the opposite side of a fountain which sprayed water from a marble urn. It required no more than a quick glance to know that these

ladies were of the haut ton. Their rings alone would
have brought enough to feed a village for five years.

"Now behave yourself, Countess," he cautioned.
"These ladies are three of the patronesses of Almack's. They can send you packing to the Colonies with
little more than a lift of the shoulder."

The countess sucked in her breath. "Dear me, yes.
Emily, that's a girl. Stand up straight and don't, for
heaven's sake, let them know we don't recognize them."

That Emily did recognize them was of little consequence. They had no reason to remember her. She and
Henry had rarely participated in London Society.

The most attractive of the three women took James
by the shoulders and kissed his cheek. "James, you bad
boy. Where have you been these past weeks? I've sent
two—no, make it three—invitations for you to attend
parties at my house and you've turned them all down."

"Princess Esterhazy." He bowed. "Truth be told, I
have been far too busy. But if I were able to accept any
invitation at all, it would surely be yours."

Countess Lieven, a pixie-faced young woman with
cropped, very curly hair peeking from below the brim
of her straw bonnet, stretched her long, elegant neck to
look in his direction. "Lord Berrington, what are we to
do with you? Almack's is such a bore without you there
to amuse the young ladies. You are, you know, our
most entertaining and eligible bachelor."

"You flatter me, as always, madam. I hardly count
myself as a jack pudding sort of fellow, or the catch of
the Season. In truth," he continued, shooting a dark
look at Lady Marguerite, "there are those who have
repeatedly called me dull."

Countess Lieven touched his arm. "I would not go so
far as to call you a rogue or a rake, my dear James, but

anyone who calls you dull must not know you very well.''

The countess covered her mouth with a handkerchief in an ill-disguised snort.

Lady Jersey, a slightly older woman with wispy, fine hair, studied first Emily and then Marguerite. "Ah, James. Could it be that you have recently removed yourself from the ranks of eligible bachelors?''

His face suffused with colour. "My apologies, ladies. I am remiss in my manners. Permit me to introduce you to my guests.''

He made somewhat awkward introductions. Especially when it came to the countess, whom he introduced as Lady Marguerite, a distant relative.

Emily held her breath. She knew it was just a question of time until the countess would refuse to be relegated to the position of distant relative. But for now they seemed to be safe.

Lady Jersey, the least attractive of the three women, took both of James's hands in hers. "Lord Berrington, now that you have house guests you must certainly make a determined effort to keep up with the London Society whirl. Not to do so would be both an affront and a waste of opportunity. Promise me you will bring your...your charming guests to my weekly tea party. I'll send the invitations round today.''

James bent to kiss her hand. "Thank you, Lady Jersey. We are honoured.''

Countess Lieven, the boldest of the three women, put her hand on Emily's arm. "Lady Emily, please don't think me rude, but I've been admiring your bonnet. Would you be willing to tell me where you found such a treasure?''

"I'm flattered, your ladyship. We...''

Lady Marguerite all but shoved Emily before she could respond. "Do forgive me, my dears, but my knee is beginning to stiffen as I stand here. I fear we must continue our stroll or I shall be forced to sit down."

Countess Lieven glanced from Emily to James to the old countess. "I see." She spoke with an icy edge. "Then may I say I look forward to seeing the three of you on Friday?"

"Friday?" Emily asked.

"Lady Jersey's tea party. Anyone who is anyone will be there."

James took Emily's arm. "I think you can rest assured that we will be there." He shot a look at Lady Marguerite. "Unless, that is, Lady Marguerite finds that her knee becomes too painful for her to attend."

The countess delivered a quelling look. "Suffice it to say, James, that I will be quite recovered by then." She smiled engagingly at the three women. "I trust that my *son* will open his house one day soon for a rout or a musical evening of some sort. In the meantime, Thursday is our at-home day."

"Your son?" all three women demanded with obvious interest.

The countess smiled. "Dear me, did I say that? Well, I've left the cover off the pot. It was to be a surprise, but the secret is too good to keep. James is my son. You see I was lost at sea when our ship went down nearly seventeen years ago." She sighed. "But Providence ruled and at last I found my way home."

James at first looked horrified by the countess's revelation, but he gathered his wits about him and rested his hand on Marguerite's arm. "Ladies, I do apologize for Lady Marguerite. She has had a very long and taxing journey and is apt to say whatever comes into her head. However, there may be some truth to what she says and we are investigating, I assure you."

There were polite murmurs all round, but there was no doubt in Emily's mind that several outrageous versions of this particular on-dit would be circulating about London before the afternoon sun had set.

James was furious as he escorted the two women back to the phaeton. "I thought we had agreed that you were to be introduced to Society as a distant relative."

The countess leaned over and tapped his chest with a white-gloved forefinger. "I should think, James, that you are old enough to have learned that one lie simply leads to another. We shall have to tell them the truth eventually. Better to have done with it at the outset rather than to make explanations later which would only serve to embarrass us."

James looked more helpless than ever now that the hot skillet was back in *his* hands. Emily tried desperately to hide her amusement.

"The harm's done, my lord. I venture to say this is our first and last attempt to make our grand entrance into Society. They are sure to turn thumbs down, but it makes no sense to worry over it."

The countess chuckled. "Don't be too quick to place a wager on it, my girl. Curiosity is a marvellous attraction. I have no doubt that we will be besieged with invitations before the week is out."

And the countess was right. Each day the silver Wellington tray in the grand entrance was filled to overflowing with calling-cards. Hardly a family of any consequence was willing to pass up the opportunity to make the acquaintance of the crazy woman who pretended to have come back from the dead.

James was appalled, Emily was amused, and the countess was delighted, but not at all surprised.

On the second day after the promenade in Hyde Park, Emily and the countess were going over the newly delivered cards. "We must select with care, Emily, my dear, before we accept invitations. Of course the patronesses of Almack's will be our first choice. Without a bid we might as well retire to the hinterlands for the remainder of the Season." She spread out the cards in the shape of a fan. "Then we shall arrange our visits in order of rank. Oh, dear. We don't need these four cards. They belong to people in Trade." She tossed the cards over her shoulder and onto the floor.

Emily stooped to pick them up and dispose of them when she recognized a richly embossed card with the signature of Mr. Grimstead, the man who wanted her sent to prison.

For one dreadful moment she thought her heart would cease to beat. Had he found her? Did he know where she was living? She had to leave, escape before he could send his toughs to capture her. She tried to stop her hands from shaking but to no avail.

"Ex—excuse me, Countess," she murmured, and fled from the room. She had just climbed the stairway to the next floor when James, with his unerring knack for further complicating her life, collided with her.

"What the—? Hold on, now. What's happened?" He held her at arm's length as he studied her face with undeniable concern. "Are you all right, Lady Emily?"

"I . . . yes, of course. Excuse me, I—"

James knew he should release her but he liked the way it felt to hold her. It made him want her arms about him. He started to pull her closer, but the expression in her eyes stayed his hands.

"My lord, please let me go," she begged.

"Not until you tell me why you are in such a hurry."

Emily willed her heart to slow down. It didn't help, having him hold her like this. It sent a multitude of conflicting messages through her head. The sensible part of her brain warned her that Grimstead could be there at any moment. The womanly part of her wanted nothing more than to stay nestled in the warmth and safety of James's embrace. Finally, the warring factions compromised and Emily's heartbeat slowed.

She managed to laugh. "It's nothing, Lord Berrington. Forgive me. I apologize for my unladylike behaviour."

James relaxed his hold on her. "No need to apologize. But you still haven't explained why you were in such a tilt."

Emily cast about for a believable excuse, but nothing came to mind. She was tongue-tied.

Only a blind man could have missed that wild look in her eyes. James's memory flashed back to his schooldays when the headmaster had forced him to stand in a corner despite the frantic call of nature. Of course. Emily was too much the lady to say anything. He'd once known a woman who died of a burst bladder rather than tell her driver she needed to stop at the necessary. Swallowing a curse at his own stupidity, he let her go so abruptly that she nearly fell. As she caught herself, the calling-cards went flying across the floor.

"My apologies, Lady Emily. I meant no offence. Go, please. I'll pick up the cards."

"Never mind," she said, scrambling to retrieve them.

"It's no trouble, I assure you." He bent down to rescue one from beneath a Queen Anne table set against the wall. "This is the last one, I believe." He held the card between his thumb and forefinger just for an instant before Emily snatched it from him.

"Thank you," she said, then turned and marched towards her room. Once inside, she closed the door quickly behind her and leaned against it. "Glory! What next?" she moaned aloud. Had he read Mr. Grimstead's name on the card? Of course Fate would have it that it was the one card he would stop to read.

She began pacing the floor, then flopped in a chair near the window. What ever was she to do? If she left quickly she might have a chance to escape. She could return to her attic room. The rent was still paid for several more days. But how long would it be before Grimstead found her there?

Once her initial fright subsided, Emily weighed her chances and considered her immediate danger. Why had Grimstead sent his card instead of simply coming after her? He was the kind of man to wait in the dark and waylay her with a gang of toughs. He certainly wouldn't forecast his move by sending a calling-card. No, this ploy was too subtle for that loggerhead's brain. She smiled. Not only that, in order to protect herself she had used her maiden name when she applied for work at his tailoring establishment. Chances were he had no idea of her true identity.

She leaned back. It was all right, then. She was still safe here at Berrington House. Safe, at least from Grimstead. But was she safe where the master of the house was concerned? She could understand and, yes, perhaps even sympathize with the cautious instincts which had caused him to question her. But why had he released her so abruptly when she failed to explain why she had been running to her room?

Then the realization struck her. "Dear heaven," she murmured. "He must think me a country dolt. How can I ever face him again?"

It occurred to her later that she needn't have been too concerned. At dinner that night, the countess was so full of herself and the plans for the impending parties that she hardly left room for an exchange of even the most mundane of explanations or pleasantries between Emily and James. Gowns, slippers, shawls, fans, and hats took over the conversation whenever the countess was in the room. James tried to look interested, but his gaze kept going back to Emily. She knew he wasn't thinking about past embarrassments or even buttons and laces, at least in the same way that the countess had in mind.

As they sat catercorner from each other across the table and listened to the countess chatter, Emily's hand went unconsciously to the top button of the rose-pink gown she was wearing. James stirred in his chair. She looked up to see him loosen his cravat as his gaze caught the movement of her hand. Emily quickly returned her hand to her lap. The countess droned on.

"And I have decided to wear the topaz-and-emerald lavaliere for our party on the twenty-fifth. James, I hope you'll be good enough to get it from the vault."

He laid his fork down on the plate with undue force. "Be careful, Countess. Do not push me too far."

"And don't you continue to be so tiresome, James. It is an unimportant piece of jewellery, but it will set off my brown velvet rather handsomely. And as our host, you can surely see to it that the necklace is safe." She leaned her elbows on the table and smiled mischievously. "Besides, I found my keys where I left them in the hollowed-out book of verse in the library. Had I wished to, I could have opened the vault and removed the jewellery myself."

James stiffened. "Then why didn't you?"

"Why, indeed? The thought crossed my mind, but it did seem a wee bit presumptuous, even though the collection does belong to me." Before he could protest, she held up a blue-veined hand. "All of it except for the blue star-sapphire-and-diamond ring, which belonged to your grandmother on your father's side. I recall that she willed it to you to give to your fiancée."

Emily looked quickly at James. If ever she had wondered about the word *consternation*, she saw it now, written all over his face.

CHAPTER EIGHT

PLACING BOTH HANDS on the table in front of him, James rose sharply and shoved his chair backwards. The footman jumped to assist him, but James motioned him away.

"If you ladies will excuse me, I'm afraid I have lost my appetite." He bowed and strode from the room.

"Oh my!" the countess said, pressing her palms together in front of her. Her mouth curved upwards with irrepressible humour. "I do believe I've unsettled the dear boy."

"Does that surprise you?" Emily demanded with a decided edge in her voice. "Sometimes I think you deliberately bait him."

The countess motioned delicately with her hand. "But it's such a challenge, isn't it? James has always been stuffy and rather pretentious. It does him good to have his ears tweaked now and then."

"And I warrant it gives you great pleasure to do it?"

The countess smiled innocently. "Who should do it, if not I?" She sobered. "What a ridiculous question. To you, of all people."

"Me? I don't know what you mean."

"Don't play moon-witted with me, Lady Emily. I saw how browsick you were all the while he was traipsing round the country—and you left behind to tend house."

"If I appeared dejected it was only because I felt the need to resume my life where I left it the day you walked in and took over."

"Fie! You give an old lady too much credit." The countess motioned to the footman that she was ready to leave. "But think how much better off you are now than you were before I decided to take you under my wing." She ignored Emily's shocked disbelief. "Don't bother to dissemble, my girl. You haven't the talent for it and it doesn't become you. Now, if you don't mind, I'll just take a glass of sherry or perhaps a wee decanter along with me and retire to my room."

Emily didn't bother to rise or in any way acknowledge the woman's departure. She sat for a few minutes hoping to sort out her own conflicting emotions. Finally, the decision made, she got to her feet, plucked a pale yellow rose from the vase, and nodded to the servants to begin clearing the table.

Just as she expected, she found James in the library thumbing through an old journal. He started to rise when she entered, but she motioned him to remain seated.

"I hope I'm not intruding, Lord Berrington."

"Hardly. I'd welcome anyone who could take my mind away from unsolved problems."

"The countess?" she asked, taking a chair near the desk.

"Who else? It was amusing at first, crossing swords with her."

"And with me?"

He smiled crookedly. "And with you, my lady."

"But now you find it . . ." she prodded.

He rubbed his fingers across his eyes and over the bridge of his nose. "I suppose I was trying to fool myself, thinking we could keep her little charade private. Now that she has made a public announcement, the game is bound to lead to chaos.''

''Then you still don't believe her?''

''Not a bit. Do you?''

''I . . . yes. I confess that I do believe the countess is your mother. There are just too many bits of evidence which seem irrefutable. I can't think of anything she hasn't explained away. If not at once, then a short time later.''

''Um. Precisely! Give her time enough to consult with someone and they find an answer to anything.''

''But who are they?''

James swore an oath, then looked apologetic. ''If we knew that, my dear Emily, we would know the entire truth.''

She looked up quickly when he spoke her given name. The warmth in her eyes was equalled by the upward curve of her mouth and her sudden intake of breath.

James was elated but hastened to protect himself. ''Surely we know each other well enough to defy convention and address each other by our given names. It's not as if we were children, Emily. Besides, I have kissed you.''

She felt the heat suffuse her face. ''Really, James. The formality of good manners was created to avoid just such familiarities as . . . as uninvited intimacies.''

''Uninvited? Perhaps, but need I remind you that you returned the salute?''

''You see?'' Her elegant nostrils flared. ''No gentleman of breeding would remind me of such an unfortunate fall from grace.''

"Personally, I considered it not so much a fall from grace as a most fortunate *saving grace*. If truth be told, I hope it happens again soon."

"You are incorrigible, sir." Emily rose abruptly. "I came in here to talk about your mother, Lord Berrington. I had hoped, now that she has told us how she refrained from helping herself to the jewellery in the family vault, that you would realize she is indeed who she says and is quite trustworthy."

He chuckled. "Give the old girl credit for her cleverness, my lady. It may be true that she found the keys to the vault in a book in the library—a hideaway even I was not privy to. That can easily be explained away by the fact that she has spent a great deal of time browsing among the books."

"Yes, I grant that she could have discovered the hiding place by accident. But if she is a thief, as you have tried so hard to convince yourself, why didn't she open the vault and steal the jewels?"

James punched the air with his forefinger. "Because I had the lock changed the day after the two of you arrived here. Point made?"

"Yes. Yes, I'm afraid so." Tears gathered in her eyes. "Why, why is it that for every step we take forward, we seem to slide backwards in threes?"

"I don't see it that way at all. Have you looked in the mirror lately, Emily? You are not the same person who confronted me in my own house nearly two weeks ago. I thought then that you were one of the prettiest women I had ever met, but when you came downstairs this evening, it occurred to me that your beauty is only equalled by the coming of spring after a long winter."

She hesitated for a long moment. "You are too kind, my lord. I hardly know what to say, except that I owe you a great deal for all that you have done for us—for me."

His pulse quickened. "What have I done for you besides taking you away from your own life? Where would you be, what would you be doing at this very moment if you had not become involved with the countess?" He tried without success to keep the intensity from his voice, but Emily noticed it at once and became wary.

"I suppose I would be at my room, reading perhaps, though the light was not very good, or preparing to retire."

"Tell me what your life was like after your husband died."

Emily stiffened. "It was empty. I cared deeply for Henry. He was the last of my family. I really prefer not to talk about it if you don't mind."

"Sometimes talking helps to ease the pain. Where did you live? *How* did you live? Did you make friends?"

"I rented a room in London," she said, aware that she had responded in a like manner to the same question when she first arrived. He was devilishly clever in his efforts to unearth her secret past, but at all costs she must not let him know about Grimstead.

She forced a smile. "As far as friends were concerned, I had acquaintances but little time or energy to make lasting friendships. Then, too, those of the working class find it hard to trust someone whom they suspect of being nobility, even though one's actual circumstances may be far worse than theirs."

"How ever did you manage to support yourself?" He felt the muscles of his face contract as he leaned forward. "I would not look askance at you, Emily, if you admitted to having a protector."

"I told you before that I had no protector. If you think so little of me as to imagine that I would stoop to such measures, then I must remove myself from your presence." She stood. "Since you are so determined to know, I found temporary employment as a seamstress."

His breathing returned to normal. He got up and went over to stand near her. "I fail to understand why you are so reluctant to talk about it. It is an admirable, though difficult profession."

"And it is no business of yours, Lord Berrington."

James saw that she was ready to take flight. He caught her hand in his and held it. "Everything about you is my business, Emily." His gaze burned into hers with such fierce heat that she felt her mouth go dry. And then he seemed to relent. "However, because you find it so unsettling, I'll not pursue the subject."

She relaxed visibly and he felt the tension leave her hand. He cupped it between his and stroked her palm with his forefinger. "Will you play for me again tonight? The harp and its music become you."

She would have much preferred it if they could have simply remained standing there with her hand nested in his warmth, but she nodded once. "What would you like me to play, James?"

His eyes darkened. "Play whatever you like, Emily." He knew he wouldn't hear the music over the pounding of his heart.

BEGINNING at an unspeakably early hour the next morning, Fredricks was summoned repeatedly to the front door to receive calling-cards and invitations from some of the most influential families in London.

Emily and the countess responded to a good two dozen of them, just enough to ensure a steady stream of guests on Thursday—guests who held the proper credentials. The countess was ecstatic.

"Emily, I do believe we are going to be the hit of the Season. I counted two duchesses, three ambassadors' wives, two princesses—not to mention Princess Esterhazy—and a dozen or so lesser members of the nobility among the cards."

"Rather good for our first at-home day, don't you agree?"

The countess considered for a moment. "Quite good, actually, though I mark it a loss not to have an opportunity to entertain Lady Cowper or Lady Jersey." She frowned. "And we still have not received our bid to Almack's. I was absolutely certain it would be forthcoming by now."

"From what I hear there is little to do at the assemblies but consume stale cakes and weak lemonade while standing elbow-to-elbow quizzing about nothing more important than scandals and fashions."

The countess looked stricken. "But what else is there, my dear? Almack's is the centre of the haut ton."

Emily's voice was dry. "I suppose we could take membership in a Society for the aid of chimney-sweeps or the organization to pursue female rights, or open a home for foundlings, or..." She threw her arms open wide. "Or rescue the cats that roam the Haymarket mews."

"Oh, do be serious, Emily. If our bid goes unaccepted we might as well... No. I won't even entertain such a hideous thought."

Emily sobered. "Forgive me. I know how important this is to you."

"Not just to me, my dear, but to James and his future wife. It is my duty to see that they take their proper place in Society. Everything depends on it."

"Considering the attention you've attracted so far, I doubt you'll have any difficulty."

"Nonsense. You haven't the least idea how it works. The attention, as you put it, is only out of curiosity to see an old woman who has come back from the dead. We need something else, something to set us a notch above all the other women who would go so far as to poison their own children for a bid to Almack's."

The countess was so overwrought that Emily cast about for something to distract her. "You haven't forgotten Lady Jersey's tea on Friday, have you? We must decide about our hats."

"Indeed. It's to be held in her garden, I'm told. Hats! Oh, my dear! We'll need something extraordinary. I think perhaps we should visit the *plumassier*'s. W.H. Botibol in Oxford Street is said to have a marvellous selection of ostrich and fancy feathers as well as artificial flowers."

"James said that we should buy ready-made bonnets in the interest of saving time."

"Fie! None of the bonnets I've seen in the shops can begin to compare with those we decorated ourselves." She pulled the bell cord. "I'll have Emmet—oh dear, I mean Fredricks—send the carriage round in an hour."

Emily sighed. She would far rather have spent the day reading or repairing the tatted lace on an ivory fichu or helping Yvette with her music. It was amazing how much the girl's singing voice had improved in just a half dozen lessons. But shopping entertained the countess, and it was a relief that she was no longer dispirited.

Surprisingly, James elected to accompany the women to the shops. As the carriage rolled along the streets, unusually uncrowded for that time of day, Emily studied his face. What had made him decide to join them? Was he afraid they would charge too much to his account? Not likely. He had scolded her more than once for remaking the old gowns in the attic instead of ordering dresses made from new materials.

James saw her watching him and it was almost as if he were reading her mind when he spoke. "While we're here, let's stop at the dressmakers. Regal Gowns is only a few minutes distant."

Emily's breath caught in her throat. *Grimstead's shop.* Did James know something? Was he trying to force her to confess that she was deeply in debt to that scoundrel, Grimstead? She struggled to keep her voice light. "What brought Regal Gowns to your mind? Are you familiar with the shop?"

"I can't say that I am. I merely recall a mention of the premises."

The countess looked interested. "Indeed, Lady Harrowby told me that their gowns are of exceptional quality. They are a little dear, I'm afraid, but one must expect to pay for the best. Suppose we stop there on our way home. We both could use something light and airy as the days become warm."

Emily stiffened. She was sure to be recognized. If she were, it would be the end of everything. She would never see James again. It took all of her self-control to smile. "What a lovely idea, James, but do you think we have enough time, Countess? We have our at-home tomorrow, and if we hope to have the hats ready to wear by Friday we must make use of every minute."

"I fear you are right, Emily. We'll just have to postpone the shop to another day."

Emily slowly let out her breath. James gave her a curious look but she managed to put him off with a smile.

Or at least she thought she had. Except for the hours Emily spent with the other women in the sewing room or alone in her bedroom, James seemed ever-present. Had it not been for her concern that he was checking up on her, she would have enjoyed his company. As it was, she felt uniquely aware of each movement she made and every word she uttered. His attention kept her constantly on guard.

"And where are you off to now?" he asked the next morning after they finished breakfast in the small morning room.

"I'm going into the garden to see if I can find some pink flowers for the large urn in the drawing room."

"Good. I'll just come along to help carry them."

"I wouldn't want to keep you from something important, my lord." Emily held out a willow basket. "Mrs. Grover found this basket to hold the flowers."

"It's no trouble. Besides, I have need of a breath of fresh air."

"Don't you have things to do? I remember that you had important letters to write today."

James grinned. "A wise man learns what tasks are truly important. Besides, I have no intention of allowing you and the countess to preside over an at-home without my being there to control things." He came to a stop near a marble bench which overlooked a pool of goldfish. "Do you find my company so unnerving?"

"It's not that I don't enjoy your company, James, but I cannot help but wonder why you seem to be watching me so much of the time." She slanted a look up at him. "Surely you are not still suspicious of me?"

He smiled. "Of course not. Have I reason to be? You've been truthful with me, have you not?"

Emily winced. It was hard to answer him and not tell a direct falsehood.

He opened the French doors and they walked outside to the terrace. "You haven't answered me, Emily."

She laughed but the sound was a bit hollow. "I assure you, James, there are many things you don't know about me, things I would never tell anyone. Such as the first boy I fell in love with, my first kiss, what it was like to be married to Henry. If I do withhold a portion of my life, it has nothing at all to do with you. Just as your personal life has nothing to do with me."

"Hmm. I wonder. Aren't you the least bit curious about whom I see and where I go when I'm not with you?"

"As to whom you choose to see, I admit to being curious, but I would never presume to question you."

He nodded. "In that respect we are not alike. I would not hesitate to ask you. For myself, I have been known to keep the company of several debutantes. Safer than seeing only one. Eager mothers haunt the marriage market, don't you know."

"Really?" Emily bit her lip to keep from asking but it didn't help. "And have you chosen one candidate in particular, or are you hoping for a harem?"

"I'm afraid I'm not ready to commit myself to that style of existence. I haven't the time for it."

She raised an eyebrow. "It seems to me that since your return we've hardly been apart. Your time must be of less value than you think."

"Does it distress you, our being together?" She hesitated, and he put his hand on her shoulder. "Now be truthful, Emily."

"You know very well that I enjoy your company, at least when we avoid subjects that are too personal, or discussions about your mother."

He stroked his chin. "You would bring up that particular burr under the saddle."

"How long can you go on pretending that she's a fraud? You surely must admit the possibility that the countess is exactly who she says she is."

"If there ever is a time to admit it, I'll be the first to let you know. I do admit that the tales she has told of the shipwreck and the years she spent getting back to London, all sound possible, though highly improbable. I also admit that I was very young when I lost my parents and I don't remember them as well I ought to."

"You see? You are very close to coming to terms with it. Why can't you just say the words?"

He sank onto a stone bench and drew her down beside him. "The truth is, Emily, that I don't *feel* anything for this woman. If she were my mother, I would have been drawn to her from the moment I saw her."

He leaned forward and pointed to a mother duck and the brood of golden ducklings which followed her across the grass to frolic in the pond. "See there? If you put a dozen female ducks in a pen with those baby ducks, they would still return to their own mother. There's something to be said for instinct."

Emily was appalled. "Instinct! Is that all that's holding you back? Great glory! I can't believe my ears. What about all the children who grew up as foundlings, never knowing that they were living with substitute parents?"

"It's not the same thing. If she were my mother I would know it."

"It's not possible with a closed mind."

James frowned. "My mind is receptive to any intelligent conversation. I think this particular subject is best left alone."

"I couldn't agree more. It doesn't change the fact that you are wrong."

His frown deepened to a scowl. "I thought you were going to cut flowers."

"Pink ones. These are all yellow and orange."

"I think there should be some pink flowers in the border near the juniper maze at the side terrace."

"Is that your instinct speaking?"

"You're very amusing today, Lady Emily. I trust that you will control your caustic wit once our guests begin to arrive."

She smiled. "Perhaps I should leave the polite conversation to your mother."

He groaned. "I'll sit next to her. You keep your eye on the sherry decanter. With enough help from the staff, we may just get through the afternoon without causing a major scandal."

THE STAFF, under the careful supervision of Mrs. Grover and Fredricks, had cleaned and polished every inch of glass, wood, and silver until the entire ground floor sparkled. Fresh flowers filled the vases and the mingled scents of rubbed beeswax, crushed cinnamon, and lemon oil drifted on the air.

At the last minute, Fredricks summoned the uniformed footmen to assemble for a final inspection. He turned to Emily. "Madam? Do you have any further orders?"

She composed herself. "Thank you, Fredricks. I believe we are ready to receive." He all but clicked his heels as she nodded and turned away. More and more, she thought, the servants were beginning to look upon her as the lady of the house. She knew it was unwise to allow herself to become too comfortable, for how long could this last?

From the moment the guests began to arrive, Emily, James, and the countess were inundated with carefully guarded questions. Surprisingly, the countess kept her counsel and refrained from making outrageous statements. James stayed close by her side and was able to redirect the conversation whenever it came too close to the enticing subject of the shipwreck. At the beginning, he had established the fact that he was trying to humour the countess, out of consideration for her age and infirmities. That seemed to satisfy everyone for the time being.

When the last guest had departed, the countess flopped down in a chair and signalled for a brandy. "My dears, I think we made great progress today. Unless I've missed the mark, I warrant we'll receive our vouchers from Almack's by messenger tomorrow morning."

James whispered behind his hand. "And so begins the demise of another great institution."

Emily shot him a dark look. "The countess behaved very well today."

"Except for the tale she told about the night she spent in a bagnio after someone gave her a wee sip of Blue ruin." He snorted. "A wee sip! I'll warrant she stole the bottle and drank it down in a single gulp."

"James, you can be so unkind." Emily could not suppress a laugh. "Tell me you've made it up. She didn't really say that, did she?"

"Upon my word as a gentleman."

Emily looked up from lowered lashes. "An ambiguous answer if ever I heard one."

The countess rose a bit unsteadily. "What are you two children whispering about? Is it the brandy? Don't despair, son. I've limited myself to two. We have work to do if we are to finish the hats before the tea tomorrow at Lady Jersey's."

James disappeared for the rest of the afternoon while the women, along with Yvette and Penelope, worked in the sewing room. The countess had purchased a large basket full of plumes, ribbons, and enough silk flowers to be used with any combination of colours they might devise. Yards of veiling filled another basket, along with a selection of undecorated straw or felt hats and bonnets.

The following day, for the tea, the countess chose to wear a close-fitting bonnet with a brim which swept high above her face. She had edged the inside border with yards of narrow, moss-green ruching that had required most of the previous day to hem. On the underside of the brim she had attached bunches of yellow silk roses in full bloom. The outside of the bonnet was covered with a thin layer of sheer veiling in a shade to match the ribbon. It narrowed at the base to tie in a bow beneath her chin. The bonnet contrasted nicely with the darker green of her gown, which was piped in a muted yellow-gold.

When James saw Emily coming downstairs dressed for the tea as well, he was enthralled. She looked more like a girl than a woman once widowed. Her lavender gown was one he vaguely remembered seeing when he was a child.

She saw him watching her. "Is it my hat? Is it too much, do you think?"

"It's perfect," he said, studying the wide-brimmed straw. "I can't believe that those are the same silk violets we bought at the *plumassier*'s just yesterday."

"They are quite real-looking, aren't they? It's the fern I'm worried about, though. Is there too much of it bordering the flowers?"

"I told you. You look perfect." He felt his chest begin to constrict when he reached for her hand as she alighted from the bottom step. "I remember that dress, or at least I think I do. My mother wore it to a party the day before they left on their voyage."

Emily heard the tightness in his voice and mistook it for pain. "Oh, James. I'm so sorry. I had no idea it would dredge up hurtful memories."

He cleared his throat. "Not at all. It is only that I am constantly amazed by your skill with a needle, not to mention your loveliness."

She reluctantly retrieved her hand. "May I return the compliment?" she said, seeing how debonair he looked in his pearl-grey skintights and matching waistcoat.

He grinned. "Are you complimenting my adeptness with the needle?"

She smiled. "I was merely thinking that even Beau Brummell would not hold a candle to you today, James."

He bowed. "I'm speechless, Lady Emily."

"And so formal."

CHAPTER NINE

LADY MARGUERITE was in something of a dour mood by the time their carriage pulled up to the door of the Jersey residence. Emily and James came to the conclusion that her lack of enthusiasm was due to their having failed to receive their bid to Almack's. Neither of them, however, was so unwise as to mention this unbelievable oversight.

But from the moment the gold-liveried footman announced their arrival, her good humour seemed to burst into bloom. Although nothing had been said, it was clear that the countess, Emily, and James were to be the recognized, if not honoured, guests at Lady Jersey's garden party.

The crowded drawing room and terrace, which extended into a manicured garden, were filled to near capacity with men and women resplendent in their best finery. Even the servants, who numbered one for every ten guests, were groomed to perfection. Chinese parasols drifted like multicoloured lotuses over a sea of strollers across an open stretch of lawn.

The countess elbowed Emily. "Look round, my dear. I'll venture to say there's not a hat or bonnet here that can compare to ours."

Emily agreed. Apparently, so did some of the other ladies, because it wasn't long after introductions were made that the compliments began accumulating along with sly questions as to the precise location of the shop where the bonnets were purchased. The countess was quick to turn the conversation in another direction.

They had been there only a short while when a young and dazzling red-haired debutante, who had been staring at them for some time, managed to slip away from her chaperon and approach them. Lady Griswold, who had for the past twenty minutes been entranced by Lady Marguerite's story of the shipwreck, reluctantly recognized her.

"Miss Mockerby."

She flashed a blinding smile. "Lady Griswold. I couldn't leave without paying my respects to everyone."

Everyone, in this instance, obviously meant James. Not once during the somewhat lengthy introductions did she remove her adoring gaze from his face.

"Oh, you needn't introduce me to Lord Berrington. The truth is, we know each other very well indeed."

James had the decency to blush. He bowed. "Miss Mockerby. It's a pleasure to see you again. Is your father well?"

"He is in good health once again, but his temperament is less than pleasant since you have neglected us so badly these past two weeks."

"I can't imagine he noticed my absence, considering how you've dragged him into the social whirl of your come-out."

She pouted demurely. "That is precisely the reason we missed you, sir! Don't pretend not to know that you are one of the most eligible bachelors in London. And don't forget that you promised to take me to Countess Lieven's Roman Ball."

James's face drew a complete blank. "I must apologize, Miss Mockerby. I don't seem to recall...."

Emily was fast becoming annoyed. Intuition and the trapped expression on James's face led her to believe that the Mockerby creature had made up the promise out of whole cloth.

Emily took James by the arm in a gesture of possession. "James, dear, how could you be so insensitive as to forget? Of course you may accompany us to the Lieven soirée, Miss Mockerby. Lady Marguerite, James, and I will be delighted to take both you and your chaperon in our carriage."

Miss Mockerby looked considerably less attractive with her jaw dropped halfway to her knees. When she was finally able to close her mouth she smiled sickly. "You are right, of course. I'm sure it was I who forgot. I do believe it was Lord Clarendon who made the promise. If you'll excuse me." She dropped a frantic curtsy and spun away in a flurry of white muslin.

The countess looked at Emily with a new sense of awareness. "Good work, my girl. I didn't know you had such pluck."

James ran his finger around the edge of his high starcher as his colour slowly returned to normal. "Uh, ladies, may I freshen your lemonade?"

The countess smoothed her gloves over her hands. "No, thank you, James. It does leave something to be desired, doesn't it? I believe I will approach the duchess, who seems to be wilting a bit in the sun."

James nodded. When she was gone he turned to Emily. "More lemonade?"

Emily impaled him with her eyes. "Did you or didn't you?"

"Do what?"

"You know very well what I mean. Did you invite that little chit to Countess Lieven's ball?"

"I assure you, I did no such thing. And I do owe you a favour for having got me out of an embarrassing situation."

"Consider yourself lucky that I didn't find it necessary to pour my lemonade in your lap."

"What reason could you possibly have for such untoward behaviour? Oh!" He grinned. "I do believe you're jealous, Lady Emily. Is this the way you plan to behave if I look at other women?"

"Only if they happen to be young enough to be your daughters."

He stroked his chin. "I see. In future I'll make it a point to ask their ages. In point of fact, I seem to remember that you are—"

"I believe I'll have that lemonade now, Lord Berrington, if you please."

He grinned, bowed, and took her glass from her hand. She tossed her head to hide her smile, then strolled away in the direction of the yew hedge.

Countess Lieven intercepted her before she had gone halfway. "Lady Emily, how lovely to see you again. And the, uh, countess? Is she with you today?"

"She seems to be entertaining the duchess with some of her tales of the shipwreck." Emily smiled. "I can always tell by the dramatic way she uses her hands to describe it."

"Fascinating." She fondled a diamond bracelet which must have weighed heavily on her left arm. "Shall we stroll?" She didn't wait for Emily to respond, but linked arms with her. "I wonder if you have any idea what a sensation the two of you are creating."

"I suppose it is rather unusual to have someone claim to have returned from the dead."

"Oh, flummery! I wasn't referring to that. I admit she is a curiosity, but everyone knows your countess is missing a few links in her chain. I was referring to your hats. They are quite the best I've seen this side of Paris. No, I confess to finding them superior even to the few French chapeaux we've managed to buy since the war began."

"You are too kind."

"Not at all. But I am persistent. Now that I have you out from under the eagle eye of Lady Marguerite, perhaps you will be generous enough to tell me exactly where you bought such exquisite creations."

Emily sighed. "You know she will never forgive me if I tell you."

"Of course. I could hardly blame her." Countess Lieven twirled her Chinese parasol. "I am most discreet. She wouldn't have to know that you told me."

Emily laughed. "Under the circumstances, I think she would know."

"I see. Would you consider vouchers to Almack's as a fair exchange?"

"Surely you jest," Emily said, with the proper amount of shock tingeing her voice.

Countess Lieven laughed. "Of course. We both know that to barter is too, too provincial."

Emily nodded and smiled. "I was told you have an infinite capacity for making mischief. It seems the gossips were right for once."

"A bit of mischief adds spice to one's life as well as complications."

"Then far be it from me to add to your complications. If it means so much to you, madam, of course I will tell you. The truth is that Lady Marguerite and I, along with two of our maids, created the hats and bonnets ourselves.''

Countess Lieven's face hardened. ''Surely you don't expect me to believe such an outlandish story? And I thought the shipwreck was a bizarre tale!''

''Would you care to join us one day? I assure you, it is a very pleasant pastime.''

''I have no talent for stitchery. I leave that to my servants.''

''Of course. But what a shame. I think you would enjoy it.''

Countess Lieven laughed. ''If truth be told, I didn't take you seriously. If you truly mean it, would you mind if Lady Jersey joins us? It seems I owe her a rather large favour. This would more than repay her.''

''It would be my pleasure.''

''When? Tomorrow?''

Emily laughed. ''If you like.''

James arrived at that moment with his hands full of lemonade glasses and a plate of sweetmeats. ''So there you are. I thought I'd lost you. Countess Lieven, how nice to see you.''

''And you, James. You haven't forgotten my party.''

''That would be impossible.''

''Then I look forward to seeing the two of you...and your mother,'' she added with a decided twinkle in her eyes. Before James could correct her she moved towards another group of strollers.

When they were comparatively alone James studied Emily's face over the rim of his lemonade glass. ''Quite the little manoeuvrer, aren't you?''

''I beg your pardon?''

"I was approaching from the other side of the hedge when I heard you finesse her into putting your names up for bid at Almack's."

Emily was wide-eyed. "Really, James, I did no such thing. Your imagination is equalled only by your..."

"Charm?" He grinned.

"Oh! You are quite impossible. Go and flirt with your little debutante."

"I think our time would be better spent looking for my—the countess."

Emily grinned. "I knew it. You're weakening."

"Don't waste a wager on it. It was a mere slip of the tongue."

It was more than twenty minutes before they could make their way through the crowd to where the countess was holding court with a large group of people. She was in her element at last, but when she saw Emily and James she rose and made her excuses.

Taking them aside, she spoke softly. "I believe the time is right for us to take our leave."

"But we only arrived an hour or so ago," James said.

The countess gave him a dry look. "Be sensible, James. We can create more of a sensation by leaving now than by waiting until the party runs down. Correct?"

James looked at Emily. She laughed. "I'm ready whenever you are."

THE VOUCHERS FOR ALMACK'S were delivered by uniformed messenger that same night.

It was not until the next morning that Emily had the courage to tell the countess that the Ladies Lieven and Jersey would be joining them in the sewing room that very afternoon. Fortunately, the countess was too ecstatic to make much of a fuss over it. But even Emily was not prepared when the ladies arrived somewhat apologetically, with a dowager duchess and a marchioness in tow. It seemed that a number of debts were due to be cancelled before the day was out.

At dinner that night James told the countess and Emily that it had sounded as if a flock of starving turkeys had roosted in the sewing room.

The countess looked more than a little smug. "Men never understand these things, James. To be among the celebrated in today's Society one must keep in step with the latest news."

"Gossip," he amended.

She sniffed. "If it were a group of men talking at White's or Watier's, you would call it a political discussion."

"As well it would be. Now, then. Are plans well under way for our small dinner party?"

Emily assured him that the invitations had been sent and accepted and everything was going as planned.

He broke a muffin in two and placed a generous dollop of apricot jam on it. "I've arranged for a musician to entertain us for a little while after we join the ladies in the drawing room."

The countess made an obvious effort to stay awake. "Excellent, my boy. Is it Bernatelli, the violinist?"

"No, Countess. I'm afraid he passed on some eight years ago. I've spoken to a Mr. Winslow de Grath, who is considered a rather decent singer. He plays the pianoforte as well."

Emily was pleased. "I think that's a wonderful idea, James. It should make the evening a little less difficult."

He looked concerned. "Are you uneasy, Emily, over the prospect of acting as hostess?"

"It's not being hostess. It's being *your* hostess that concerns me. There are those who will attach more importance to it than is due. It could cause a great deal of gossip, you know." She glanced over at the countess, who was nearly asleep. Emily lowered her voice. "It really should be your mother sitting in the hostess's chair."

James scowled. "We'll not go into that. If they want to talk, then let them. We should have grown used to it these past weeks. When the evening is over I'll count us lucky if they are talking about us instead of the countess."

As Fate would have it, on the twenty-fifth nothing turned out quite the way it was planned. The countess was suffering a miserable sore throat, the musician was waylaid and injured by a cutpurse, and a new servant had spilled furniture oil in the centre of the best full-length tablecloth.

James was distraught. At her wits' end, Emily dispatched him to his study, sent the countess to bed under Millie's watchful eye, cut and fringed a running length of bright linen to cover the spot on the tablecloth, then sent the servants scurrying to pick daisies for nosegays to be placed at each setting. The entertainment was another problem.

James strode across the room and back. "It doesn't have to be anything elaborate. It's not as if we require an orchestra or an ensemble. All we need is a musician to play for a short time while we assemble in the drawing room." He slapped his hand against his forehead.

"Of course. Why didn't we think of it? You can entertain us on the harp."

Emily was appalled. "You can't be serious. I only know a few simple pieces."

James waved her protests aside. "I'll leave it to you. You still have three hours before the guests are due to arrive."

"Your confidence in me is overwhelming," Emily said dryly.

"Yes, it is," he said. His eyes held a smouldering look that was becoming more familiar to Emily as the days went by.

"Oh, James!" she wailed.

"Yes?"

"Oh, never mind. Go and see that the stable-boys are ready to tend to the carriages."

How she managed to pull everything together at the last minute, Emily later couldn't remember. As luck would have it, the countess escaped Millie's watchful eye and appeared just in time for dinner. But the most difficult part was yet to come. Emily had just finished playing a simple folk song on the harp and was waiting for the mild applause to end. James was beaming, but the smile turned to a look of pure confusion when Emily nodded and Yvette walked hesitantly into the room.

She was like no Yvette James had ever seen. Instead of the plain grey-and-white uniform, she wore a saffron gown cut low in front to show a lovely if somewhat enticing display of creamy shoulders. Her timidity only added to her appeal. She moved towards Emily as if she were walking in a dream. It was only then that James recognized her as the upstairs maid.

"What the..." Emily heard him say under his breath.

She smiled with more assurance than she felt. "Ladies, gentlemen. May I present Mademoiselle Yvette Corday." There was an expectant hush. Emily whispered reassurance to Yvette. "Pretend we are practising alone in the music room. Put your hand on the music rack if you need support."

Yvette smiled stiffly and Emily began the opening strains. At first the girl's voice lacked strength, but as the music swelled, her confidence grew and the melody floated up, pure and sweet.

When she finished, the audience applauded with genuine appreciation and begged for more. Yvette looked questioningly at Emily, who said, "I suppose we might try 'The Nightingale's Lament.'"

"*Oui*. And then perhaps 'The Shepherdess's Song.'"

Emily smiled. "I learned recently that it is important to leave while everyone still wants more."

"*Oui. Certainement!* I understand." She took her place and inclined her head briefly as if she were about to address a group of adoring friends. It occurred to Emily as she strummed the opening passages of the song, that this was precisely what was happening. Yvette had made her mark. Her life was sure to undergo some remarkable changes.

Later, Emily realized that she had underestimated the effect Yvette had on James's guests. They insisted on hearing two more songs, and it was only Emily's insistence that she was not adept enough on the harp to be able to accompany her which finally persuaded them to let her go.

James was jubilant. "Lady Emily," he announced as the last guest departed, "you are a treasure." He turned to the countess, bowed, and kissed her hand. "And you, madam, were most cordial and attentive during the entire evening."

"Why thank you, James. It was a lovely party, my dears, but I do have the most insignificant complaint. Really, James, you must do something about your wine cellar. The burgundy the footman poured for me was really quite off."

James straightened. "I say! Is that true, Emily? I thought mine was superb."

Emily's face froze. "The bottle used to serve the countess was perhaps of a different vintage. I'll see to it tomorrow."

The countess lifted a decanter from a table. "No matter. Since everyone seemed to be enjoying theirs I thought it best not to comment. I'll just take the sherry up to my room and have a wee nip before I retire."

When she was safely out of earshot James took Emily by the arm. "And what, may I enquire, did you give the countess to drink for dinner? It couldn't have been wine. She didn't fall asleep over her soup."

"It was just a simple decoction of fruit juice laced with a few herbs which are guaranteed to have a soothing effect on one's nerves. I thought that she would possibly not notice."

"Not notice? My dear Emily, the countess has wine for blood. I'll warrant she has consumed everything from West Indies rum to the finest French champagnes."

"Not to mention Blue Ruin and Strip-me-naked."

"How could I forget?"

"But she behaved beautifully."

"And so did you, Emily," he said, drawing her close. "You were the perfect hostess." He brushed a kiss against her forehead. "Except for one thing."

Emily met his gaze. "And what was that?"

"Just that you nearly gave me heart failure when Yvette walked in without her feather duster."

Emily grinned. "She was good, wasn't she?"

"Too good. I saw the Baron Falkenheim asking her to sing at the reception he is giving for the Duke of Evanstoke. I think you will need to hire another upstairs maid before the year's end."

Emily moved a safe distance out of his reach. "The task of hiring maids should be yours, James. After all, it is you who must live with her. I shall long before then have returned to my own life."

"Don't even think such a thing. My house could no longer function without you."

"You give me too much credit. Mrs. Grover does an excellent job. All she requires is an extra hand or two to assist with the heavier work. There are many fine household workers for hire."

"You know that I wasn't talking about housework."

"Do I, James? Once you tire of the game you play with the countess and decide to cast her into the street, what excuse will you find to keep me here in your house?"

He stepped closer. "I wasn't aware that I needed an excuse."

She moistened her lips, which had suddenly become dry. "Or you may relent and admit that the countess truly is your mother."

"That would require a miracle."

"And you don't believe in miracles."

"Some, but not that particular one. For example, I would consider it a miracle if I can restrain myself from taking you into my arms."

"No! You mustn't do that."

"Does the thought displease you so?"

She moved farther away from him. "You know that it doesn't. But why begin something that has no hope of surviving? You still don't trust me, James, and I confess that your inability to recognize the countess as your mother gives me cause to wonder about your fairness."

He had started to reach out to her but he dropped his hands. "Upon my word, Emily, you can't hold that against me. If I were only able to believe it, I would be the first to admit that she is my mother. You speak of fairness. What more can I do that I haven't already done for her?"

"Oh, James. I'm so sorry. You're right, of course, and I do beg your forgiveness. You have been more than generous to both of us. Nevertheless, my life has not been easy this past year and I must begin to look to the future." She sighed. "But for now, I really must say good-night."

He wanted to vow to love and keep her forever, but somewhere in the back of his mind the thought still nagged that she was hiding something from him. He swore an oath as he watched her glide down the hall. If it was the last thing he did, he'd find out what it was.

THE DAYS WHICH FOLLOWED seemed to merge into one another. Emily had taken Mrs. Grover's suggestion and dosed the countess with a concoction of lemon juice and syrup made from the bark of wild cherry trees to relieve her sore throat. Whether it was the medicine or plain determination, the countess recovered without missing a single party or rout.

Moreover, the twice-weekly hat-making sessions had expanded to include two more ladies of the haut ton.

Although the participants endeavoured to keep it a secret, once they began wearing their singular creations, every woman of fashion made it her mission to discover their source. The countess was in her glory.

It was the week of Countess Lieven's Roman Ball. Emily had been working for days on the gown she hoped to wear, an airy thing, all froth and lace which drifted over her figure like silver-blue sea foam. The gown was cut in the Grecian mode, high-waisted and draped to reveal one bare shoulder. Since the weather was still cool in the evening, she found a long, flowing coat of silver satin lined with blue satin a few shades darker than the dress.

The countess surveyed it with a critical eye. "The flowers on the coat are too much. You need something simple. A jewelled clasp or a fancy button. Perhaps we can find something at Cyril Montague's new shop."

Emily was more than reluctant to face the crowds at the popular new shop, but the countess persisted. Something odd had been going on between James and the countess since breakfast and Emily was nonplussed. He readily agreed to escort them, adding the suggestion that they stop afterwards at Halliburton's Tea Room.

Not only was James becoming less cautious about taking the countess out in public, he seemed to be creating opportunities for the three of them to be seen together. Was it part of the game that he continued to play?

From the moment the carriage pulled up in front of Montague's shop with its white stone pots filled with red geraniums, James seemed to be sitting on the edge of his seat. The countess, too, appeared wound a little too tightly for her spring. Emily had a premonition that something was dreadfully amiss, but she took James's hand to alight from the carriage and allowed him to guide her into the store. There was scarcely room to move, but the countess elbowed her way towards the back.

It was then that Emily saw him. First it was just a glimpse of his beaver top hat which triggered her recognition. It was an unusual hat, with its gold cord edging the top and brim. French made, it was not of current fashion, but a hat which Mr. Grimstead favoured over all others. She shrank back against James, who was following the countess in the general direction of where Grimstead stood.

"What is it?" James asked. "Are you all right?"

"I...the truth is, I feel a little faint." It was too close to the truth. Had James and the countess somehow discovered her connection to Grimstead and brought her here to meet him? Not likely. There would be no purpose in that. Still, if they continued as they were, their paths were sure to cross.

James looked worried. "Here. Lean against me. We should have listened to you and stayed home. You've been working too hard."

"It's not that. It's the crowd, I think."

He held her in the curve of his arm. "Your colour is off. I'm taking you back to the carriage."

He summoned the countess, who looked a little provoked at the change in plans. "Go ahead with her to the carriage. I'll tend to our little chore and join you in a few minutes."

James looked sceptical about leaving her alone in the store, but did so to avoid an argument.

Once inside the carriage he took Emily's face in his hands. "There. You look much better. You frightened me half to death, Emily."

His obvious concern touched her, but if she allowed him to continue in that vein... She made an effort to smile. "All I needed was some fresh air. We shouldn't leave the countess unescorted."

"Right." He spoke to the driver, then got up. "I'll just see to her and be back at once."

Emily leaned her head against the plush cushion. Grimstead had given her quite a start, but she was safe. He hadn't seen her. Dear heaven, when would she be rid of him? If only she had the courage to tell James. But to do so would be to risk losing his respect. Not only that, but Grimstead had vowed to take revenge on the other seamstresses if she ever caused him trouble. Those poor women. How could she put them at risk? Her only hope was to somehow find the money to repay him, or depart London for some place where he could never find her.

Her thoughts were interrupted by the arrival of James and the countess. Neither of them spoke much on the way home but the current of intrigue between the two of them was as thick as smoke from a waterfront manufactory.

CHAPTER TEN

ONCE THEY ARRIVED back at the house in Mayfair, Emily had handed her cloak to Fredricks and started for the stairs when James apprehended her. "If you can spare a few minutes, Emily, I should like to see you in the library."

Something about his tone sent a shock of warning up her spine. She looked at the countess, who collected her parcels from the footman and disappeared down the corridor to the library.

"What is this, James? What's going on? I know there is something between you and the countess."

A muscle quirked at the side of his mouth. "You have such a suspicious mind. I have a bit of news for you." He looked down at her, noticing how innocent and vulnerable she was in spite of her apparent strengths. Her eyes reminded him of those of a young doe about to take flight. "God's truth, Emily. You look terrible. I didn't mean to frighten you."

"I'm not fond of surprises, James." She tried to keep her tone light, but the ever-present fear that Grimstead would come after her was too intense.

"Must you always be on guard? From the moment you arrived here you've been looking behind your back. What is it, Emily? Let me help you."

She laughed a little hollowly. "Speaking of suspicious minds, you still haven't told me your news." She stopped abruptly. "James! Is it possible you've found the proof that Marguerite is your mother?"

"No, not quite." He nodded to the footman, who opened the door to the library.

The countess was waiting inside near the long table, her parcels still unopened. She smiled at James. "Will you go first, or shall I?"

He bowed. "Ladies first, Countess."

"Of course. Very well. Emily, my dear, this is for you." She handed her a wrapped package. "Open it. I can't wait to see your face."

Emily looked from one to the other. Too uneasy to say anything, she carefully opened the paper and lifted the lid from the box. "Slippers! In the exact shade to match my new gown." Her eyes misted. "I don't understand. What is the occasion?"

The countess brushed a kiss against her cheek. "Simply a token of our love, my dear. We had them made especially for you."

"They're lovely. I—I can't thank you enough. Both of you."

James cleared his throat. "The slippers are from the countess."

Emily thanked her again and kissed her on the cheek.

James handed Emily a small, square, velvet-covered box. "This gift is from me."

Emily looked up sharply. "What is it? I can't accept—"

"Of course you can. Don't refuse it until you see it."

She removed her gloves, then lifted the lid of the box and turned it towards the light. Inside was a pearl-and-diamond clasp and a matching pin mounted in silver filigree. She looked up at James, who was smiling widely, and shook her head. "You can't mean this for me."

"I can and I do."

"But I can't accept such a costly gift."

The countess tilted her head back and looked up at her. "Don't be a ninnyhammer. Of course you can. Thank the man and be done with it, Emily."

James grinned. "For once I have to agree with her."

Emily brushed at her face with the back of her hand. "Thank you, James. I will treasure them always. They will go perfectly with my new coat and gown."

"Precisely what I had in mind, but hold on. Is 'thank you' all I get? I believe a kiss on the cheek would be in order."

Emily blushed becomingly and glanced at the countess, whose efforts to look sober were obviously in vain. "Well, go on, my girl," the countess said. "You don't need my permission."

James offered his cheek and Emily brushed it lightly with her lips. "Thank you, James," she said softly.

He cleared his throat. "The pleasure was all mine, milady."

Later, in her room, Emily had to admit to a mild disappointment. For one bizarre moment she had thought he was going to ask her to marry him. The thought was ridiculous, of course. He had everything to offer her and she had nothing. Society would never forgive him for wedding a pauper, and a widow at that—particularly one who faced debtor's prison. She held the clasp in the palm of her hand and the pearls seemed to take on an even warmer lustre.

THE DAY OF THE ROMAN BALL drew near. The women were gathered for their Wednesday afternoon hat-making session when Lady Marguerite adjusted her spectacles on the end of her nose and confronted Countess Lieven.

"Dorothea, my dear. Will the Prince Regent be in attendance at your soirée?"

There was a gasp followed by a dead silence. Then Countess Lieven smiled sweetly. "Dear, dear Lady Marguerite. I thought everyone knew that the Tsar and the Regent were at swords' points with each other. It would be foolhardy to put them in the same room." She twirled a dark ringlet around her forefinger, drew it across her chin, and smiled mischievously. "So I've invited the Regent's wife instead."

A gasp went up around the long table. "Dorothea, you haven't!" Lady Jersey said. "You know what Princess Caroline is like. Granted, she's very popular among the people since the Regent cast her out, but think of the repercussions."

"Precisely, my dear," Countess Lieven rejoined. "I confess that I rather like the woman. In her own way she is quite fascinating." She screwed up her face and puffed her cheeks into a near likeness of the German-born princess. "*Mein Gott*, vat a goot und heppy party ziz vill be."

The women dissolved into laughter, in spite of the fact that most of them sympathized with Princess Caroline and deplored the ill-treatment she had received during her unhappy marriage to the Prince Regent. Caroline was out to get attention, and she was, they all agreed, presently racing headlong downhill in a barrel of her own making.

Later, Emily told James what had happened. He replaced the quill in its holder and slid some papers into a drawer. "Nothing surprises me where the princess is concerned. The Regent was ill-advised to marry her. Caroline is cut from cloth a little too coarse to be royal." He closed the drawer and locked it. "Since their official separation she has been living at Kensington Palace, but the prince is doing his best to declare it a hotbed of Jacobinism and close it down."

"Then why would Countess Lieven invite her to the ball?"

"Vengeance, I suspect. She would do anything in her power to stir up trouble for the prince, considering the ill will that has been brewing between him and the Russian Tsar."

"Then you think there will be trouble?"

"Only time will tell."

WITH TWO SMALLER PARTIES and an assembly at Almack's to attend before the Roman Ball, Emily had precious little time to worry about Countess Lieven's mischief-making. And there were other things to see to.

One afternoon, when the countess was napping and James was attending to business, Emily ordered the carriage brought round. The rent money was running out on her room and she was forced to make a decision. She hated to risk discovery by returning to Meecham Street to collect her few possessions, but the time might come when she wished she had them. Besides, it was only fair to let the landlord know that she was leaving.

The landlord had already answered her knock when she realized that she was too well-dressed, considering that just a few short weeks ago she had been poverty-stricken. He squinted at her through eyes which were faded blue and inflamed.

"'Tis you, Mrs. Merriweather," he said, using her maiden name, which she had given him. "The missus was worried after you."

"Thank you, Mr. Jepson. It was kind of your wife to be concerned but I'm quite well."

"Aye, I kin see thet all right."

"I am returning the key. My rent is paid through tomorrow but I'll not be needing the room again, at least for a while," she amended.

"You've come into money, then?" he asked, pulling a dirty stocking cap from his equally grimy hair.

"I'm staying with a friend."

"So that's the way it is." He all but snickered. "There was another of your *friends* enquirin' after you a few days back. An' right eager to find you, 'e was."

Emily winced at the way Mr. Jepson said "friend". She fixed him with a cool gaze. "Did he leave his name? Can you describe this person?"

"'E left no name. 'E was fleshy about the belly and face. Wore a fine top hat, though, with fancy gold trim. Not a true gentleman, to my way o' thinkin'."

"May I ask what you told him?"

"There was nothin' to tell. Is it some kind o' trouble you're in, missus?"

"Of course not. The person in question is a nuisance, nothing more."

"'E said 'e'd be back."

"Just tell him I've gone away, if you please."

The landlord sucked on his teeth. "Mayhap I could remember if you gave me a little somethin' to smooth the way."

Emily sighed and extracted a coin from her reticule. "That's all I have, Mr. Jepson. It will have to do."

The disappointed expression on his unshaven face gave her little hope that he would do as she wished, but she turned and left him standing in his doorway.

When Emily arrived back at Berrington House, James was already home. She was summoned to the library. He rose to meet her at the door.

"Where have you been? Don't you realize what harm you can do to your reputation by going out unescorted in the afternoon? You should have asked me first."

"I didn't know I needed your permission."

"God's truth, Emily! I swear you delight in twisting my words. Of course you don't need my permission to use the carriage. I was worried about you, that's all. My driver is experienced but a woman alone is too much responsibility to place upon him." He wiped his hand across his face. "Just where did you go?"

"I went to my old room to collect my belongings. My rent was paid only through tomorrow."

"I would have gone with you."

"I wanted to go alone."

"Secrets again, eh?"

"Just a part of my life that doesn't concern you."

"But I *want* it to concern me."

"I'm sorry. This is the way it has to be."

"What are you so afraid of? Tell me. I swear I can fix it."

"No one can. It's best forgotten."

He gripped the back of a chair. "Did you kill someone?"

"Oh, James! How can you say such a thing? Don't you know me better than that?"

"I've been trying to get to know you, but I've weighed everything else in my mind, and nothing, short of murder, is so vile that you would be afraid to share it with me.''

He took her hand and held it between his palms. ''Emily, I care for you. I won't let anything happen to you. Tell me.''

Tears gathered in her eyes and she shook her head.

James looked at her for a long moment, then lifted her face to meet his and kissed her long and thoroughly.

It took all of her willpower to break away from him. Only after she dredged up the sly face of Mr. Jepson and his crude insinuations was she able to step back.

Her hands were shaking as she brought them to her cheeks. ''Please, please. Don't do this to me.''

James's face turned white around the mouth. ''My apologies. Am I to understand, Lady Emily, that you do not return my deep affection?''

She reached out to touch him, but drew back at the last minute out of fear that she could no longer restrain herself. ''I would be less than honest if I said I didn't care for you, James. But encounters like this can only lead to trouble. Though I cannot presume to know what is in your mind, I can only state that I am in no position to agree to an alliance. Of any kind,'' she added as an afterthought, since he had yet to suggest marriage.

He was silent too long. She picked up her gloves and reticule and walked towards the door. At the last minute she turned to say something, but the distress in his eyes stopped the words before they escaped. *Don't let him say anything now,* she prayed. All she wanted at that precise moment was to be alone in the sanctuary of her room.

It was with an overwhelming sense of loss that James watched her go upstairs. Why hadn't he told her then and there that he wanted to marry her? All his life he had been forced to say the correct words, do the proper thing to protect his title and the family name. Having been orphaned at an early age, he had had to work twice as hard to understand his responsibilities and to do what was expected of him. Why couldn't he simply marry the woman—and her reputation be damned? He swore softly. He would find out where she had gone today. His driver would tell him or live to regret it. It would be a start, anyway. Maybe it would even be the key to unlock Emily's past.

FOR THE NEXT TWO DAYS Emily saw little of James. When he joined the women for dinner it seemed as if his body were present but his thoughts were elsewhere. Apparently the countess noticed it, too, because as the carriage approached the Lieven mansion on Harley Street the night of the Roman soirée, she leaned forward and put her hand on his knee.

"James, my boy, it is so good to see you smile. I thought for a while your ill humour would never end."

"I've just been preoccupied. But I assure you, Countess, that nothing will distract me tonight, with two such beautiful ladies to grace my side."

The countess smiled. "In truth, I feel beautiful since you saw fit to let me wear my necklace."

"May I remind you, Countess, that it is only for tonight?"

"We'll see, won't we? Oh look! They've erected a colonnade all along the drive to follow the Roman theme."

Emily smiled at the transparent way the countess had of changing the subject. She looked at James and was relieved to see that he was grinning.

It took several minutes for their carriage to reach the head of the line and for the passengers to alight. They were greeted by a double row of footmen dressed in knee-length togas and sandals laced up to just below the knee.

The house was ablaze with torches and gas lanterns set at close intervals between tall urns of greenery and potted palm trees. Low tables of food were kept constantly filled by a score of Nubian servants whose oiled skin glistened in the flickering light.

Emily handed the footman her coat and walked alongside James and the countess towards the drawing room. "I feel as if I'm in a different world."

James looked at her. "It becomes you. I like your hair wound round in that chignon with the little curls hanging down the side. Strange. Sometimes it looks more gold than brown."

The countess grabbed James's arm. "Look out on the veranda. Isn't that Princess Caroline in the purple gown, dancing with that Turk in the red turban?"

"I think so." He looked down at the countess. "Now, remember. You promised to behave yourself tonight and not say anything controversial. And don't tell any more stories about spending the night in a Turkish bath."

"James, you offend me."

"I'm only saying this to spare all of us considerable embarrassment."

"Don't I always behave with dignity?"

He was saved from having to answer when Countess Lieven descended upon them and enveloped the women in her arms. "My two favourite ladies. How good of you to come. And how handsome you look, James. If you weren't so smitten with Lady Emily, I confess I might set a trap for you myself.''

Emily was amused. "Countess Lieven! And you a married woman! You are completely without conscience.''

"Yes. Isn't it fun? Come, I want you to meet the duchess. She's been asking after you.''

Emily looked helplessly back at James as she was taken in tow, but he was already taken in hand by a bejewelled matron and her daughter.

Dorothea Lieven was wearing a sheer white silk gown cut in the Roman style, with an undergown of dampened flesh-colored muslin which clung to her shape like a continuation of her own skin. Highly fashionable, Emily decided, but with no style. She thought of Marguerite and smiled.

The theme of the party quickly deteriorated into a pseudo-Bacchanalian revel. One could hardly take ten steps without being offered a glass of wine along with thinly sliced cheese, sweet pastries, grapes, and nuts. Emily, with some difficulty, was able to refuse all but a single glass of the rich red wine. More, and she would have been sleepy. Too sleepy to keep her eye on Lady Marguerite.

The music blared forth from the veranda, which overlooked a dance floor set up in the garden. Emily had just been introduced to the Baron Von Kirken when he asked her to dance. He was a good-looking man a few years her senior, with carefully groomed blond hair that curled deliberately round his forehead. His manner was polished to a fine patina, but she was not taken with him. His attempt at seduction, for that was what it was, was a little too obvious.

When he asked for a second dance she tapped him with her folded fan. "I'm flattered, Baron, but we both know that to dance another round with you would compromise my reputation."

"Ach! In London that would be true, my lady. But look around you. Is zis not Rome?"

"Yes, indeed, but look what became of the Roman Empire, *mein Herr*."

He bowed. "As you wish." He handed her over to a dandy dressed in white satin breeches and a satin coat with heavy epaulettes. Emily had forgotten his name before the dance was over. He seemed to be intent on the quantity of partners he could claim in an hour's time.

One after another they came to fill her card. And James still hadn't asked her to dance. She saw him several times through the crowd. He looked pleadingly at her, and to give him credit, she saw that he had tried to reach her side through the crush of revellers. Defeated, he had danced twice, *twice*, with the Mockerby creature in her ruffled and flounced debutante's gown. After that he seemed to disappear somewhere into the maze which stood at the end of the garden path.

And where was Lady Marguerite? She had danced a dignified minuet with a grey-haired man of imposing stature, then had been turned over to a silver-haired gentleman in blue satin breeches and a cutaway coat with gold braid at the shoulders. Both had seemed quite taken with her.

Emily curtsied to the lieutenant with whom she had just danced. She would have gone off in search of the countess, but someone caught her arm. She turned, breathless. "James. It's you."

"Who did you think it would be? The first dance should have been mine, my lady."

"I'm sorry. You were on the other side of the dance floor."

"You could have w-waited. The next waltz is ours."

"I've already promised it to Sir Geoffrey."

"Then retract it."

"I can't. You know it would be an affront to him."

"And wh-what about me?"

"You sound like a petulant child." She looked at him closely. "Have you been drinking heavily, James?"

"Only to avoid the M-Mockerby chit. I see you managed to catch the eye of Baron Von Kirken. H-he was drooling over you like a dog on a b-bone."

"Don't be absurd. I danced with him only once."

"That was a d-dance? We thought you never stopped talking."

"We? You've seen the countess?"

"No."

"Then you must mean the Mockerby girl."

He coloured, then pretended to scour the grounds. "Sir Geoffrey seems to be d-delayed. I th-think we . . . we'd better look inside for the countess."

Emily gave him a cold look. "Indeed, that is if you can walk without falling over your feet."

It didn't take long. All they had to do was follow the noise of the commotion which came from the drawing room. At one end of the room, a gilded Roman chariot had been erected on a low, flower-covered dais. A large crowd was gathered round it, cheering and stamping their feet.

Emily looked, then looked again. "Dear heaven! I must have had more to drink than I thought." She laughed. "For a minute I imagined that was your mother standing in the chariot."

James steadied himself against a marble column. "And I thought I was foxed." He grinned, then sobered. "By all that is holy. You're right!"

Emily groaned. "Just look at her. She's brandishing that palm frond like a whip. Why couldn't she have just fallen asleep in her soup as she always does?"

As they watched spellbound, a short, stout woman in purple velvet jumped up and down shouting, *"Vite, vite!"*

The countess shook the ribbons she was holding for reins and shouted, "Giddap, giddap, you old bag of bones." At the same time she waved the palm frond in the air. At the other end of the ribbons was the white-haired gentleman with whom the countess had been dancing earlier in the evening.

Emily gasped and started to push her way towards the front. "Help me, James. We have to put an end to this."

His mouth tightened. "And once and for all."

It wasn't easy for James to follow. He found it hard to walk straight, let alone fight his way through the noisy onlookers. At last Emily reached the chariot and all but dragged the countess out of it.

She was unrepentant and provoked. "Unhand me, madam."

The woman in purple velvet stood nearby, mopping copious tears of laughter from her eyes. "Get avay. Leaf her go. *Mein Gott*, until dis voman came dis vas de dullest party vot Gott Almighty did born."

Emily looked directly at her. It was Princess Caroline, the Regent's wife. Emily paled. "James, let's get out of here."

He looked a little unsteady, but he managed to take the countess's other arm and turn her in the direction of the door.

"W-wait up, I say." The countess giggled. "We can't leave without me trusty steed." She burst into a gale of laughter which brought an echo of merriment following behind them. James was too befuddled to concentrate, so it was up to Emily to order their carriage brought round. She didn't wait to make her apologies to Countess Lieven.

Once they were settled in the carriage James and the countess fell to discussing the party. One thing led to another, and before Emily knew what was happening, the two of them were regaling each other with anecdotes. As for Emily, she was not amused.

A carriage followed them closely for some distance, and it occurred to Emily that the countess must have made a favourable impression on her silver-haired comrade in comedy. Nevertheless, she was glad when he gave up the chase and they returned home without incident.

Fredricks, summoned hurriedly from some chore below stairs, made haste to assist Emily in getting the two culprits into the library. He looked affronted. "I must apologize for his lordship's behaviour, madam. It isn't like him to get in his cups this way. Upon my word, it's only the second time I've seen him foxed since he left school."

She fanned herself, feeling warm from the exertion. "I think we'll need a very large pot of coffee, Fredricks, and thank you for helping me. One is bad, but *two* drunkards are beyond the pale."

The countess fixed Emily with a bleary eye. "You were very rude not to acknowledge the Princess of Wales. Caroline was quite friendly towards me."

"C-Caroline, is it?" James said. "Next thing we know you'll be invited to K-Kensington Palace. M-maybe you can p-pretend you're the long-lost heir to the th-throne?"

"Or maybe Prinny's looking for a new wife," the countess said, grinning hugely. "I'm told he favours older women."

Emily was furious. "Listen to the two of you talk. I've never heard such nonsense. Stop it at once."

The countess and James, grinning like idiots, were slouched on either end of an upholstered settee. Emily strode across the room and moved a tall, Empire mirror so that it reflected both their images. "Look at you. It's enough to shame the devil."

The countess yawned and leaned her head back against the settee. Within an instant she was sound asleep.

James sat as if stupefied, then slowly staggered to his feet and confronted his face in the mirror. "My God! I don't believe it. I look just like her."

"Precisely, James. And what's even worse, tonight you began acting like her."

CHAPTER ELEVEN

JAMES WAS UNABLE to tear himself away from the mirror. The likeness to the countess was horrifying to him. "It's not true. It can't be true. I'd know it if she were my mother...wouldn't I?"

Emily levelled her gaze at him. "A sobering thought, so to speak. Ah, here's Fredricks with the coffee. I think you have need of it, sir."

James held the cup between his shaking hands. "I feel as if I'll awaken suddenly to find that this is all a nightmare."

"It's real, James. You might as well face it. Drinking too much doesn't solve the problem." She added more coffee to his cup. "The truth is, you haven't found one ounce of evidence to disprove Marguerite's claim that she is your mother. Why do you continue to fight it so?"

He wiped his face across the sleeve of his waistcoat. "Was it the wine or did I see her driving a chariot with Lord Denby in harness?"

"You saw it all."

He sighed with obvious relief. "Then need I say more? My mother would never have made such a spectacle of herself. She was too well-bred."

"Poverty changes people, James. She's not the same woman she was seventeen years ago."

"Has it changed you?"

"Of course it has. I had no idea the extremes people had to go to just to survive. One can't experience a life of poverty without being changed by it." A picture of the women who slaved with her at Mr. Grimstead's tailoring shop flashed before her eyes and she blinked.

James pressed his fingers against his temples. "That's quite different. Poverty hasn't changed your breeding. I could never see you behaving crudely." He took a long swallow of coffee. "I shouldn't drink red wine. My head is spinning like a whirling dervish." He stood. "I regret that I spoiled the party for you, Emily. By all that is holy, what must you think of me now?"

She took the cup from him and set it on the tray. What did she think of him? If she told him how much she had come to love him, there would be no turning back. "I think you need sleep. The countess, too. I'll have Fredricks send for your valet."

Emily took a long time undressing after she looked in on the countess and found her fast asleep and snoring. The night was still young and her thoughts too confused to permit sleep. Fredricks had prepared a small repast—a cold collation of meats and cheese along with thin slices of crusty bread. She nibbled a piece of bread and cheese as she walked to the window.

It was quiet here compared to the wild celebration that must still be taking place at the Roman Ball. She sighed. James had warned her about becoming too friendly with Countess Lieven. Her reputation was legend for her ability to manipulate people, men in particular. The Duke of Wellington had been quoted as naming her "a *femme d'esprit* who could and would betray everybody in turn if it should suit her purpose."

Emily cooled her fingers on the windowpane, then held them against her face. But, everything considered, she liked Dorothea Lieven and could hardly blame Marguerite's and James's fall from grace on anything but their own weaknesses.

Below, an unlighted carriage approached slowly down the street. Only an expertly cautious driver could handle the horses so quietly on the rough cobblestones. The carriage came to a stop in front of the house and paused briefly while a man pulled aside the curtain and looked out. Then he signalled the driver to move on. The darkness was too intense for Emily to be certain, but she could have sworn she saw gold braid on the side of a tall beaver hat.

At long last Emily fell into bed. She spent a restless night haunted by dreams of Cyrus Grimstead chaining her to the wheels of a chariot, while the countess, dressed in purple, tied James into harness with an emerald necklace.

WHEN EMILY WENT DOWN to breakfast next morning, James had already gone out.

She questioned Fredricks. "Do you know where he went at such an early hour?"

"No, ma'am. He didn't say."

"Was he all right?"

"He appeared to have completely recovered, your ladyship."

Emily wished fervently that she could say the same for herself. At a time when everything should have been perfect, her whole world was falling apart. She should have stayed with the countess last night instead of being caught up in the festivities. None of the bizarre events would have happened if she had attended to the task James gave her when he asked her to remain in residence at Berrington House. She had assumed it would be so easy to prove or disprove Marguerite's claim, but the countess's unconscionable misbehaviour last night would surely not help her cause.

Emily had just reached for a scone when James came into the breakfast room bearing an armful of tiger lilies. He clicked his heels together and bowed. "Madam, I wish to beg your forgiveness for my rudeness last night. I admit to being thoroughly scotched." He handed her the lilies. "Just a small token to express my regret."

"They're lovely, James."

"I don't know what came over me last night. Truth is, I rather dislike the taste of liquor. I never drink to excess."

She handed the flowers to a footman and looked back at James. "There was one other time, I believe."

He looked puzzled, then a smile washed over his face. "That's right. I remember it now."

"Do go on. I can't wait to hear about it."

"If you must know, I had just finished school and was ready to leave for home when I asked my French teacher to marry me. She refused. No, to be honest, she laughed at me."

"How sad. You must have been heartbroken."

"Don't sound so smug. I was devastated, in spite of the fact that she was twenty years my senior."

"But you got over her?"

"My guardian saw to it that I was kept very busy. I learned later that he had paid her a handsome sum to refuse me."

"And you never forgave him."

"Or her. At least not immediately, but I came to understand the merit of his decision. It taught me something about my responsibilities to the title and to use caution in order to keep the family name unblemished.''

"Until last night.''

"Yes.''

"What happened?''

"I think it was in part, at least, seeing the countess so readily accepted as my mother.''

"Surely there must have been more than that.''

"And seeing you on the arms of other men.''

"I know you mean that in jest, James.''

"Do I indeed?'' His eyes darkened and the tiny muscle throbbed in his right temple. He pulled his chair closer to the table. "Emily, I have to know. Do you *really* believe that the countess could be my own mother?''

"I . . . I only wish I knew. Most of the time I'm convinced she is genuine, but other times I wonder if I simply want to believe her because I like her and admire her courage and sense of humour.'' Emily sipped her chocolate and put her cup down. "I am sure of one thing. You can't continue this way for long. She won't permit it. You're going to have to make a decision either to accept or reject her.''

He shook his head. "I can't. I have too many things to decide. There is something more important which must come first.''

"What could be more important than settling accounts with your mother?''

"I can't discuss it now. I have an errand I must run before we talk about it. An errand that concerns the two of us.''

Before she had a chance to recover, he got up from the table and left the room.

Emily was stunned. James was going to offer for her hand in marriage. She knew it as surely as she knew the sun would rise the next day. But she couldn't marry him. Not without telling him about Cyrus Grimstead. And that was impossible. Grimstead had made his threats all too real.

For the next two hours Emily had trouble finding her emotional feet. One moment she was in the clouds, thinking what it would be like to be married to James. The next moment she was in the depths of despair at the thought of losing him. Her only consolation was that she didn't have to deal with the countess, who was still fast asleep.

It had been Emily's intention to write responses to notes and invitations they had received during the week, but she kept running to the window to see if James had returned. She had just taken a fresh sheet of stationery when she heard a carriage enter the crushed-rock driveway. She put her hands to her hair and wished she had time for Yvette to redo it. Instead, she pinched colour into her cheeks and smoothed the lace fichu over her pink-flowered morning dress.

The door to the library opened and Emily looked round expectantly. It was Fredricks. "Begging your pardon, madam. There is a gentleman here to see you. He is most insistent."

"Did he leave his card?"

"No, madam. And he gave no name."

"Then it would be most improper to see him. Did he state his business?"

"I questioned him, your ladyship, but he—"

There was a scuffle outside the door to the hallway and Fredricks whirled round. "See here, you can't—"

Both Fredricks and the footman tried to eject him, but he was persistent. Emily caught hold of the edge of the desk. The man forcing his way into the library was Cyrus Grimstead. She felt her knees begin to buckle, then Grimstead saw her and his eyes glittered with undisguised malice.

"Ah, there you are, madam. A word with you, if I may."

Emily felt as if her world were rushing towards a disastrous end. She had no choice but to speak with him. She nodded to Fredricks.

Grimstead adjusted his clothing and picked up his top hat, which had fallen to the floor. "A wise decision, madam. I'll not be long, but I've waited near on a month to speak with you." He lifted his shoulder in the direction of Fredricks and the footman. "Mayhap you would prefer to discuss this matter in private?" He grinned, revealing a gold tooth set in the front of his mouth.

Emily held on to the back of a chair for support. "It's all right, Fredricks. You may go."

Fredricks looked uncertain. "Perhaps I should remain?"

"No, Fredricks. That won't be necessary." The butler hesitated, but she nodded to him and the footman left the room with obvious reluctance.

Grimstead settled himself in a rosewood chair. His considerable bulk spread out beneath the delicate arms and Emily wondered if the chair would hold him.

"Now then, Mrs. Merriweather—or is it Mrs. Harding? I believe there is a matter of some money you owe me." His voice was as oily as his hair.

Emily spoke quickly in order to get rid of him before James returned. "I told you before that I couldn't pay you. You cheated me and the other seamstresses who work for you. The price you charged for the food and the miserable hovel you called a rooming-house was far too high.'' She was shaking so hard she could hardly speak. "It was morally wrong to force us to live there just to keep our positions.''

"But you did, missy. Now you owe me all the money plus thirty per cent more for the time and trouble it took me to find you.''

Emily gasped. "And just where do you think I'll get it? This isn't my house. I have nothing of my own except my clothing and a few books.''

"Then it looks to me like they'll be sending you off to Newgate Prison.'' He grinned. "Or mayhap they will transport you. Or then again, mayhap one of the guards which run the prison can find a better use for you.''

"Get out of here.''

"And give you another chance to run off? No, ma'am. I'll just wait here whilst my driver fetches the constable.''

"I need some time to get the money.''

A crafty expression flitted across his face and he stood up. "I don't trust you that far, missy. But here's what I might do. You get me some orders for gowns from your fancy friends, say about six or seven of them, and I'll consider your debt paid.''

Emily caught her breath.

He laughed and it turned into an ugly cough. "I know what you are thinking, but it won't work. I mean ball gowns—silk or satin or velvet, or maybe some o' that fine Austrian lace or French brocade.''

Emily saw his proposal as a way to gain time. "H-how do I know I can trust you to cancel my debts?''

"I'll give you my word." He laughed. "It's the only choice you have. I'll give you four weeks. If the seven gowns are ready and you have the bill o' sale with my name at the bottom, then I'll tear up your chits and we'll call it square."

"All right. I'll see what I can do."

He strode over to stand just inches away from her and grasped her fichu in his hand as if to choke her. "Now you listen here, you high-class tart. You run away again and next time I won't be so easy on you, do you hear?"

"Take your filthy hands off me."

He laughed and stepped back. "You cross me, woman, and I'll make you pay. And when I get through wi' you I'll start in on your friends—those that still work for me. Little Charity first, I think, since I know how you always looked after her."

"Get out of here."

"That I will. If I don't get some orders in a week, I'll be back." He picked up his top hat, brushed it with the sleeve of his coat, and tipped it in her direction.

When he opened the door, Fredricks, who was standing at the ready, ushered him unceremoniously towards the front entrance.

Emily closed the door and slumped against it to the floor. She pressed her hands over her face with a feeling of complete despair. Her circumstances had been bad before, but now they were far worse than she could ever have imagined. There was no hope, no hope at all, that she could survive this time.

A footstep sounded in the room and she started. James was standing beside her. He reached for her hands and lifted her to her feet.

"Oh! James. You frightened me." She tried to pull away but he held her hands in his.

"Why didn't you tell me?"

"Tell you?"

He swore softly. "Don't dissemble, Emily. The time for games is over." He jerked his head towards the rear entrance to the library. "I heard everything. What's more, I know this man and the scoundrel that he is."

"Oh, James. I didn't want you involved in this. What can I do?"

"I'll pay him off. The money is all he wants. He's in dire straits and needs to repay some gambling debts."

She was appalled. "How do you know that?"

"I've been asking questions about him."

"Why would you do that? What does Cyrus Grimstead have to do with you?"

James grasped the front ends of his waistcoat and assumed his stubborn look. "He had nothing to do with me until I saw the calling-card you dropped in the hallway. His name had a frightening effect on you so I was convinced he had something to do with your past." James's gaze softened. "I won't let him hurt you, Emily. Let me take care of your indebtedness."

"No, James. I couldn't let you take on my debts."

"You can't stop me." He reached out to her and held her face in his hands. "Be truthful, Emily, for God's sake. Was this the terrible secret you've been keeping from me these past few weeks?"

She nodded. "He threatened, if I told anyone, he'd take out his revenge on me and on the other women who still work for him. I can't let him do that. He'd send them to prison or sell them into slavery to the Turks." The tears which welled in her eyes threatened to spill over. "Don't you see? I can't just pay him off and go on my merry way. For one thing, I don't think he'd let me off so easily." She dabbed at her eyes with a lace handkerchief. "No one ever gets away from him, James. I want to see him punished and those women set free to find decent work."

"How many women are there?"

"Nine, when I was there. Seven of them are girls but two are old women. I don't know how long they can survive."

James pulled her close. "Leave it to me. I'll take care of it."

Emily clung to him for a breathless moment, then pulled back. "I know you mean well, but how can you help? There's nothing you can do. If you just go rushing in headlong to confront him, it will be the women who pay."

James gave her a long, slow look. "Give me credit for a little sense, my dear. There are a dozen ways to win a war. I think I inherited my mother's instincts for survival."

"Your mother's . . ." Emily let out a shriek. "James! Are you saying what I think you are saying? Have you decided to admit that the countess is your mother?"

He sighed. "Almost. I have consulted with barristers and talked with scholars. No one seems to agree on what I should do. But just between the two of us, I have nearly decided to welcome the countess home."

"Have you told her?"

"I'm not quite ready to do that. I thought perhaps we should have a ball and make a public announcement. I think she would prefer a rather extravagant surprise party over a simple acknowledgement."

Emily leaned forward and kissed him on the cheek. "Yes. The countess would love it. Oh, James! I'm so very happy. You won't regret it."

"I will, you know. About five times a week. Every time we have to rescue her from the punch bowl or drag her back from some outrageous escapade."

Emily sobered. "We? I can't remain here any longer, James. Surely you must realize that."

"As my wife you can go or stay anywhere you wish."

She looked up at him. Her hand trembled and her voice shook when she spoke. "How I wish it could come to pass, but we both know it can never be."

"I love you, Emily. I have since the moment I saw you."

She smiled. "At Heatherwood Castle? I think not, James. You were too smitten with the Russian servant girl."

"Um. I'd forgotten. But isn't it about time we made up for those lost years?"

She hesitated. "You know I love you. Too much so to let you take over the responsibility for my problems. No, James, I can't do anything until I find some way to resolve my situation with Cyrus Grimstead."

"Then it's time we began making plans. He's given you a bit of a reprieve before he makes trouble. Let's use the time to set a trap."

He bent down and kissed her. For a few precious minutes Emily gave herself over to the wonder of loving and being loved.

James brushed the top of her head with his chin. "Now try to tell me we aren't in this together. From now on, Emily, whatever we do, we do as one."

"I can't promise, James. I need time to think about it."

"You've already had five minutes. I consider that quite enough. Do you agree?"

"I—I agree. On one condition: that we keep this to ourselves until I've settled my grievance with Cyrus Grimstead."

"Then let's make it happen soon, my love."

THE PLANS BEGAN to take shape that very afternoon. They included the ladies of the Wednesday afternoon hat-making club, which now consisted of Countess Lieven, Lady Jersey, the Duchess of Annesley, the Marchioness of Southfort, Elena, Baroness Trapham, and Mrs. Clive Fanhurst and Miss Amelia Trotter—two lesser-known ladies of the ton who had only recently developed a fondness for needlework. They also happened to be women to whom favours were owed by Lady Jersey and Lady Trapham.

To make the plan work it was necessary to inform the ladies of exactly what was going on. At the next meeting of the hat circle, James explained how Emily had become involved and what they must do to put Grimstead out of business. It all revolved round the soirée that James, with Emily's help, planned to put on at Berrington House.

Lady Marguerite looked up from the embroidered hat she was making to go with her flowered silk. "A party, James? How wonderful. I trust there will be dancing?"

"Of course." He looked sideways at her. "But no Roman gladiators and absolutely no chariots!"

She dimpled. "Would you consider a one-legged gardener hitched to a dogcart?"

Everyone laughed. Countess Lieven shook her head. "My dear Marguerite, I fear I have corrupted you beyond hope."

"Don't flatter yourself, Dorothea. I knew about such things long before you were born."

Countess Lieven inclined her head. "Touché, my dear. I admit to believing you."

A look passed between Emily and James. They both smiled, and Emily knew that he was thinking about how surprised Marguerite would be when she eventually learned that the party was also to be in honour of her return home.

The women were delighted to become part of the intrigue, but Emily seriously wondered how good they might be at keeping the secret. For secret it must remain if the plan was to work. When she expressed her fears to Countess Lieven, the pixie-faced woman curled a glossy black ringlet round her finger.

"You have nothing to worry about, Emily, my dear friend. I warned the ladies that if anyone so much as whispered a word of our plan, she would be banished from our hat club. There isn't one member who wouldn't die rather than disclose our plans. Now then, James, when do we meet with your Mr. Grimstead?"

"Tomorrow. We have no time to lose. You will go to his place of business, no more than two at a time, and order gowns to be made for the party. They must be kept simple, because of the time involved, but they must be of the most expensive fabric you can find."

The women twittered at the thought of indulging their fancies. He shushed them with a smile. "Now, be certain to say that Lady Emily Merriweather Harding recommended his shop most highly. And also make certain you say that your gown is to be delivered on the twenty-third. No sooner, no later."

Lady Jersey finished stitching a row of pearl beads on the brim of a lace hat and clipped the thread with a pair of tiny scissors shaped like a stork. "I have only one objection, Lord Berrington. It does seem such an imposition to allow you to pay for these gowns. You know that each one of us can well afford them."

He inclined his head. "I am well aware of that, Lady Jersey. Consider the gowns a gift, a small token of our appreciation for helping us send a scoundrel to gaol. I can't think of a better way to spend my money."

It was with a growing sense of respect that Emily watched James take command of the situation. It seemed that nothing was left to chance. A man was sent to spy on Grimstead in order to know what nights he would be absent from the shop. As Fate would have it, he spent every evening at the gambling dens near Fives Court in St. Martin's Street, the Thatched House Tavern in St. James's, or Daffy's Club in Holborn. James and Emily chose a night several days after this pattern had been established and Grimstead was known to be at one of his haunts, to visit his employees.

A feeling of dread washed over Emily as they climbed the dark, rickety stairs to the rooms where the women lived above the store.

James sensed that she trembled. "What is it, Emily?"

"Memories. I spent the better part of a year slaving away in this place. Even so, I came out the loser in the end when Grimstead tallied my bill for room and board."

"Don't think about it. Try to remember we're going to put an end to it, not just for you but for all the women he has indentured."

"I hope so, but I am beginning to have doubts."

"Steady, my dear. It will be over before you know it."

Emily was comforted just hearing his voice, but when they reached the top of the stairs, James brushed her cheek with his fingertips. She could feel the warmth of his breath fan her cheek.

"Trust me, Emily. I promised I wouldn't permit anything to go wrong."

She nodded. "Then I suppose we had best go inside."

Looking back on it, Emily was both amazed and surprised by the way everything went. Had it not been for James, the plan would have been defeated before it began. The seamstresses—only eight of them now, for Catherine had passed on—were understandably suspicious. The years of mistreatment they had suffered had done little to encourage them to have confidence in anyone who professed to want to help them, but James won them over.

He stood before the women assembled in the cramped and dusty sewing room. "I understand your fear of losing what little security you have. But think of this: your friend Catherine is gone now. What chance do the rest of you have to escape from Grimstead before you suffer a similar fate?"

A murmur went up. A cough punctuated the ripple of voices and silenced them. They knew Maria would be the next to leave them. Her cough worsened each day.

Charity lifted her wide, brown eyes. "But what will happen to us with Mr. Grimstead gone?"

James spoke gently. "Can you be in worse straits than you are now? I can see to it that you remain living here without charge until you find other employment. I give you my word. I can't promise to make you rich, but I swear that when this is over, you will be far better off than you are now."

No one answered. Emily's stomach began to flutter. Then Flora pushed herself to a standing position. "Aye, an' I do trust ye, Lord Berrington. I'm wi' ye, for good or no."

Priscilla sighed heavily. "As we all are, your lordship. I didn't think I could work any harder than I already do, but hope is a powerful medicine. That's what you've given us."

CHAPTER TWELVE

RACHEL AND FLORA, the only two of the seamstresses Grimstead allowed downstairs in the shop, reported that all the members of the hat club had ordered gowns to be finished and delivered on the twenty-third. Grimstead was so overjoyed that he had turned away less lucrative jobs in order to complete the gowns on time.

James nodded. "Precisely what I had hoped. The plan is already under way. Are you willing to help us?"

They all nodded their agreement.

James smiled. "It's done, then. I'll see that the materials are delivered as soon as the gowns are cut. You must keep them well hidden when Grimstead is in the room." He linked his fingers together over the front of his waistcoat. "Remember, if your employer hears one word about this, the plan is doomed."

Polly Bander, the eldest of the eight women, pulled her woollen shawl close around her bony shoulders. "Sure, an' yer a good man to try to 'elp us this way, Lord Berrington. But then you've always been a good man from what the talk says. You can rest assured we'll not be after spillin' the beans."

Later, on the way back to the house in Mayfair, Emily leaned against James and he put his arm around her. His voice was husky. "When I think of you and those women and how Grimstead uses people, I want to kill him."

"That would be too easy for him." She reached over to stroke his wrist in the narrow place where his sleeve ended and a curl of dark hair brushed the top of his gloves. "You are quite wonderful, you know."

He looked down at her face, just visible in the flickering light from the coach lantern. "I intend to remind you of that a few years from now."

"Oh really? Am I to assume that I'll need reminding? Is it your intention to misbehave?"

"It is not my intention, my love, but I strongly suspect that we shall sometimes disagree."

Her voice was dry. "Certainly not more than twice a day. I warn you, your mother will side with me in our disagreements."

"I've no doubt about that. Unless—"

"Unless what?"

He grinned. "Have you forgotten that I hold the keys to the wine cellar?"

"You wouldn't be so cruel as to deprive her of one of life's pleasures!"

"Deprive her? On the contrary, I intend to make it my task to provide her with other pleasures. Have you noticed that when she's busy she hardly touches the sherry?"

"What could possibly make up for the loss?"

"I thought we might build a new conservatory."

"Oh, James. She would love that, but I hardly think that gardening would entirely replace her fondness for the grape."

"How about her fondness for a certain stately gentleman by the name of Mr. Harrington? Or more to the point, his fondness for her?"

Emily straightened. "Do you mean that there is something between them? I know she has leanings towards him, but I didn't know her feelings were returned.''

"Didn't you see how crushed he was while she was cavorting with Lord Denby the night of Dorothea's party?''

"All I could think of was removing her from that accursed chariot.'' Emily leaned back against his shoulder. "There is one problem, though. Your mother is very conscious of her position. Would she stoop to a permanent alliance with someone whose bloodlines are not as sound as hers? Mr. Harrington is, after all, untitled.''

He laughed. "Only she can answer that. One thing I know. If she points her finger in his direction, the poor soul hasn't a chance of getting away.''

"You admire her for that, don't you?''

"I suppose I do. It's just another facet of her personality of which I was unaware when I was a boy. I remember only one occasion when she refused to let me have my own way.''

"Dare I ask?''

"It was about a year before my parents left for Italy, when I was sent off to boarding school. I didn't want to go, but my mother told me I was going and that was that. She wanted me to grow up, I suppose.''

"Is that all? And did it help?''

He looked down at Emily and saw the faint gleam of mischief in her eyes. "Careful, my lady. You are sitting in too dangerous a position to remind me I sometimes behave like a little boy.''

"You do, you know. When you can't have your way.''

"Then we must see that I always get my way.'' He nudged her chin with his thumb and covered her mouth with his. In spite of herself, Emily responded to the urgency of his kiss. Her fingers curled in the soft hair at the nape of his neck and he drew a ragged breath.

When Emily was finally able to compose herself, she looked directly into his eyes, which even in the dim light shone with dark desire. Her voice sounded breathless. "Forgive me, my lord. I was wrong. You are no longer a little boy."

"I count the days until I can offer you further proof."

Emily felt herself blush. "The proprieties, sir. Don't forget the proprieties."

FOR EMILY, the days that preceded the party at Berrington House were filled with mixed feelings of apprehension and anticipation. The seamstresses were already at work on the dresses ordered from Mr. Grimstead, including Emily's gown of an unusually fine Chinese silk, in a rich shade of ivory shot with gold threads. Unbeknownst to Mr. Grimstead, who ordered the original fabric, James had placed a second order—enough extra material to make an exact duplicate of each of the patterns chosen by Emily, Marguerite, and the other ladies of the hat-making club.

When Lady Jersey saw the bolts of material stacked on the table in the sewing room at Berrington House, she fanned herself in agitation. "Never have I seen such a collection of fine fabric. Is it possible? Shall we be able to finish the gowns in time?"

Countess Lieven gave her a quelling look. "We said we would do it and we will. Now then, Emily. Show us what to do."

Emily saw the doubt written on some of their faces. She tried to hide her own misgivings with a show of confidence. "Don't worry. You won't have to do the hard part. I'll show you how to cut the fabric and stitch the simple seams. My seamstress friends will sew at night to complete the work. Then when the gowns are ready to be fitted, we'll see to the adjustments back here.''

The duchess shifted the heavy rings on her finger. "You know, I think this little plot against Mr. Grimstead is most exciting. I welcome the change. Unlike you, Dorothea, with your little intrigues, I've led a very prosaic life.''

Countess Lieven slanted a look across at her. ''Not as prosaic as you'd like us to believe, Susanna. Need I remind you of that sea captain you were said to have met on your last tour?''

The duchess giggled. ''Dorothea, you are wicked to dredge up old rumours.'' She picked up a bolt of green brocade. "Just for that, I insist we start on my dress first.''

The others, amused by her obvious attempt to change the subject, gathered round the table to receive their instructions. At first there was so much laughter and confusion that Emily despaired of ever getting the material cut and ready to sew, but one by one the patterns were laid out and leftover scraps of the costly fabric fell to the floor in a colourful pile.

Countess Lieven looked up suddenly from the brilliant jade watered silk on which she was sewing. "If I told the ambassador we were working as seamstresses he would never believe me." She chuckled. "Having an affair? Yes. But making my own ball gown? *Nyet!* He would throw me out of the embassy." She tossed her curls over her shoulder and looked at Emily. "As it is, he was beginning to question why I spend so much time at Berrington House, until he saw you and James in a tête-à-tête at Almack's last night. Have you something to tell us, Emily?''

Emily happened to catch a glimpse of James coming down the hall in the direction of the sewing room. She smiled conspiratorially. ''The truth of the matter is that I do have a rather important announcement, Countess Lieven.'' Emily didn't have to wait to get their full attention. She listened as the footsteps approached, then leaned forward. ''I know this will hardly come as a surprise but—''

James entered the room. ''Ladies? Am I interrupting something?''

Emily smiled sweetly. ''Not at all, James. I was just about to announce that tea would be brought in momentarily. Will you join us?''

Countess Lieven's eyes glittered with good humour. ''And they accuse me of being devious!''

THREE WEEKS PASSED all too quickly. Seams were sewn, then ripped and sewn again. Emily despaired that the baroness would ever finish the ruffles which were to edge the hem of her gown. Instead of even gathers, there were bunches of fabric punctuated by sections that were nearly flat. At her wits' end late one night, Emily pulled the threads and reworked the narrow length of fabric until the ruffles were regularly spaced.

Countess Lieven, in a sudden burst of generosity, had sent her secretary to help Emily write the invitations for the ball. They were delivered immediately and most of the acceptances had already been received.

James took Emily to visit Grimstead's shop twice more, after making certain that he was spending the night at the gaming halls. She was surprised to see how much better the women looked, until Polly Bander thanked James for the nourishing food he had provided. Emily wanted to put her arms round him then and there. A more considerate man she had never met.

The next morning he came into the conservatory where Emily and the countess were discussing flowers for the ball. He whistled softly. "I say! You've brought the place back to life, Countess. I had no idea you could force so many flowers into bloom so quickly."

"The gardener helped me. Of course he hasn't the skill of Hawkins Willoughby, but he's still young." She picked a dead flower from a stalk of delphinium. "I thought these might do well for the party. We have an abundance of them and they will look nice in the urns, combined with some white statice and some greenery. Of course we have roses and forget-me-nots for the tables."

He looked at Emily and then back at the countess. "Amazing. The two of you have brought an air of grace which has been missing at Berrington House for far too many years." He signalled to a footman, who stepped out of the conservatory, then returned a moment later bearing a flat leather case. James took it from him and dismissed him.

"Countess," James began, "I think it appropriate that you have some jewellery to wear with your new gown on the night of the ball. I've selected some rather significant pieces from the vault and I should like you to choose one. Whichever one you choose will be yours to keep."

She clasped her hands to her heart and tears welled up in her eyes. She sniffed, dabbed at her nose with a square of lace, and looked from James to Emily and back again.

"I'm touched—more than you know, James. For you to do this when you still have doubts about me is too, too precious."

Emily spoke through the tightness in her voice. "You know that we both have great affection for you, Countess."

"And it is returned in equal measure. But I cannot, James. I simply can't accept. Your offer is far too generous under the circumstances."

"But I insist."

"Very well. If you insist, I will just take this simple little strand of pearls as a token of your esteem. They will look well with my midnight-blue satin, wouldn't you say, Emily?"

"Exceedingly well."

The countess thanked him, lifted the necklace from the box, kissed James on the cheek, and left to take it to her room.

Emily came over to kiss his other cheek. "Oh, James! If I didn't love you already, I would love you now. You are so kind."

He laughed and shook his head. "That woman will be my death. Try as I might I can never outguess her."

"What is it, James? Which one did you expect her to choose?"

"Certainly not just a 'simple little strand of pearls,' as she put it. I thought perhaps something a little more sensational in appearance. The ruby-and-garnet choker, for example." He laughed. "I don't know if she was pretending ignorance, but the necklace she chose was worth more than all of the others put together."

Emily was amused. "We've never doubted that the woman has taste. I suppose we should be grateful that she hasn't asked to wear her tiara to the ball."

"Maybe she hasn't thought about it. We still have two more days." He put down the box on a table. "You look tired, Emily. You've been working too hard."

"I'm trying to hide my doubts. Sometimes I think we should never have begun this attempt to best Grimstead at his own game. It could be dangerous for so many people."

"Nothing will go wrong. With the friends we have helping us, Grimstead is already defeated." He kissed her forehead. "Two days, Emily. Two days and it will all be over."

She tried to keep that thought uppermost in her mind as she completed the hundreds of tasks remaining to be done. The gowns had been turned over to the seamstresses at Grimstead's establishment. They were amused by some of the clumsy stitches, but as in one voice, they promised Emily to finish them in time.

It was fortunate that anyone who was anyone would be at the party. Yvette had become so popular as a singer that if there had been another party that evening, chances were that Yvette would have been engaged to sing there. As it was, Emily asked her to entertain at the ball and Yvette agreed. Emily was amused and very relieved to learn that Yvette had selected a certain Mr. Waterford as an accompanist. The girl was no fool.

Grimstead's seamstresses finished the duplicate set of gowns on the night of the twenty-second. Amazingly, most of the dresses required little, if any, alteration to make them fit decently. Emily breathed a sigh of relief that the most difficult part of the plan was complete. Late that night she marshalled the ladies from the hat circle, so that the dresses could be fitted and pressed.

They were cavorting in their new gowns in front of the mirrors in the sewing room when James walked in. He stepped back in mock dismay. "'Pon my word. Is the queen holding court, or why else do we have such a bevy of beauties assembled here? My compliments, ladies." He bowed deeply and the women responded with girlish laughter.

Emily, whose gown had been completed earlier and was hanging at the ready in the armoire, pressed her hands together in front of her. "They do look lovely, don't they, James?"

The baroness flipped her skirt and twirled in a giddy circle. "Isn't it too, too delicious? I never thought we could do it."

Countess Lieven linked arms with James. "No one will ever believe that we did most of the work ourselves."

Lady Jersey giggled. "And you will make certain of that, Dorothea. What will you say? That we imported some famous couturier from the Continent?"

Countess Lieven arched her long neck. "A remarkably good idea, my dear, considering it came from you." Her laughter took the sting from her words. Everyone knew that the two women had been the best of friends ever since they, along with "Cupid" Palmerston, introduced the waltz to the scandalized dancers at Almack's.

The duchess snipped a dangling thread from the sleeve of her gown. "Now all we need is the receipts. Is that what you have there, James?"

"It is, your grace. All properly signed, as they should be." He unhanded himself from Countess Lieven's clutches and spread out the papers on the table. "Make certain that you take the receipt with your own name at the top of the order. Otherwise there could be reason for questions.''

Emily looked them over, until she found hers and the one belonging to Marguerite. She held them up and studied each in turn. "James, how did you manage this? The signature looks so authentic that I would swear it belonged to Cyrus Grimstead.''

James chuckled. "I can assure you, my dear, that it is no work of mine. As it turns out my stable-master knew just the man for us. Of course we must not speak of it outside this room.''

Lady Marguerite said, "My dear boy. You are such a wonder. I didn't believe this would work until I saw the evidence right here in front of me.''

The duchess retied a satin bow which had become tangled on a hook. "Now then, James, tell us exactly what we must do and say when your Mr. Grimstead delivers the gowns tomorrow.''

"It's very simple, your grace. All you need do is look shocked and tell Mr. Grimstead that the gowns were delivered earlier in the day, and that you have the receipt to prove that you paid the bill in full.''

"It sounds so easy but I don't see how it can work,'' Miss Trotter protested. "Couldn't we call the constables?''

Countess Lieven sputtered in irritation. "Oh, do be serious, Amelia. What could he say? That we didn't accept the gowns?'' She preened herself, running her palms suggestively down the length of her hips. "We have the gowns to show for it. Can he say that we didn't pay? We have the receipt written on his own stationery, signed with his own pen, by his own hand. More or less.'' She smiled mischievously. "Besides, what man of his class would dare question the word of ten of the most influential ladies in London, not to mention their husbands?'' She looked sideways at Emily. ''And sponsors.''

They all laughed. Emily glanced at James and blushed, but quickly recovered. She hoped it would be that easy. To be on the safe side, she warned each of the women to be sure that her servants were present when Grimstead arrived.

THE FOLLOWING DAY was the twenty-third. Emily had hardly slept at all the night before. When James came down to breakfast she confronted him.

''I've been worried sick. There is one thing we didn't allow for.''

James cupped her chin in his hand. ''The date of our wedding, perhaps? It's already arranged.''

''Oh, do be serious.''

''I am. How does one month from tomorrow appeal to you?''

''I—I don't know what to say.''

''Say yes.''

''Don't confuse me, James. I'm worried about Maria and Charity and Flora and all the other women who work for Mr. Grimstead. What will he do to them today after he learns what we did to him?''

''First, answer my question. Will you marry me next month?''

''Yes, providing that . . .''

''No qualifications, Emily. Promise me.''

She looked up at him, and he marvelled that anyone so capable and so strong could look so vulnerable and shy. ''James, you know that I love you with all my heart.'' She had it in her mind to ask him to wait for her answer, but seeing the hope written so plainly on his face, she relented. "You do me great honour, James. If it is your wish that we marry in a month's time, then the answer is yes."

"The honour is mine, Emily. I love you more than I can say. I swear I'll make you happy."

"You've already done so. But I must confess that I am worried about my friends at Grimstead's."

"Then worry no more. I've arranged for my carriage to collect them and bring them here as soon as Grimstead leaves the store to deliver the gowns."

"You're bringing them here?"

"Yes, there are some unused rooms in the servants' wing. I grant you, the quarters are not luxurious, except compared to their present circumstances. They can stay here until Grimstead is taken into custody, as I assure you he will be once his enormous debts are made public. After that, they can return to the shop and we shall see to it that they are made comfortable."

"How long do you think it will be until he comes to deliver our dresses?"

"I don't know. You can be certain it will seem longer than it actually is."

The house was nearly in order for the ball to be held the next day. Emily took charge of the dusting and polishing which remained to be done, as well as the beds which were to be made up in anticipation of the arrival of the seamstresses. She was grateful for Mrs. Grover, and Fredricks, and Cook, who knew their duties and performed them well. The house smelled fresh and airy with only a slight hint of the pastries and hams and fowl that were being prepared below stairs in the kitchen.

Three hours passed, hours in which Emily jumped each time a carriage rattled by in the street. A short time later, James's messenger arrived with the news that

Grimstead had already attempted to deliver some of the gowns and had left each house in a state of uncontrollable rage.

She was putting fresh candles in the chandelier in the upstairs hallway when there was a commotion at the front door. It took Fredricks only minutes to answer the knocker, but in that time she thought the front door would be pounded down. Her heart thudded against her ribs. This was the moment she had been waiting for, yet dreading. With a quick prayer on her lips, she steadied herself and went downstairs. James met her there.

He gave Fredricks the signal to open the door. When he did, Cyrus Grimstead shoved his way past him and confronted Emily. His face was livid.

"You'll never get away with this, you cheap little hussy! I'll have the constable after you before you can count to ten!"

Emily pressed her hands together. "Mr. Grimstead, do make sense. What has happened? Is something wrong?"

James stood off to one side. "Sit down, Grimstead. You look about to go into apoplexy. Your face is as red as an apple."

Grimstead accepted a chair the footman brought him and tried repeatedly to catch his breath.

Emily smiled. "That's much better. If it's the gowns you're worried about, both mine and Lady Marguerite's dresses fit perfectly."

He puffed out his cheeks and his chest wheezed when he tried to draw a breath. "I delivered no dresses. You and your thieving friends! You all have the same story. But how could I have delivered them? They're still in my carriage! I took no money from you!"

"Nonsense. I have your receipt, marked Paid in Full. The gowns are perfect." She turned to the butler. "Fredricks, will you send someone upstairs to fetch them for me? We must prove to Mr. Grimstead that the orders were filled as he promised. And you, Mr. Grimstead, will honour your promise to cancel my debt in its entirety."

He jumped up and lunged at her, but the footmen were ready and they restrained him. He tensed, then his jaw sagged and his hostility vanished like a gold sovereign in a beggar's fist.

"You can't do this to me, milady. You're trying to drive me mad," he whined. "If I don't pay for the cloth I ordered for the gowns, the drygoodsman will have me thrown in prison. Have mercy, I beg you."

James planted himself directly in front of him. "The kind of mercy you showed to Catherine, and Maria, and Charity, and Flora, and the others?"

Grimstead paled. "You know about them?" His eyes glittered. "Aye, play it your way if you wish, milord, but if you have any pity for those women you'll see it my way."

"The women have already left your establishment, Mr. Grimstead. And you might as well go, too. There is nothing here for you now." His eyes narrowed. "Point of fact, there is nothing for you anywhere."

They watched him slink away, a broken man. Emily stood in the curve of James's arm. "What will he do now, I wonder?"

James tightened his hand on her shoulder. "He'll run true to form: take what little money he can lay his hands on and try to recoup his losses in the gambling dens. After that it's just a question of time until the Charlies find him. We have nothing to fear from him now."

They turned and walked towards the library. "I can't believe it's all over," Emily said, leaning her head against his shoulder.

"All over? Emily, my love, it's just begun. Our guests have arrived in the servants' quarters. I've asked them to be shown to the salon, so that the countess can meet them."

"And the party tomorrow," Emily said. "After everything we've been through, I'd almost forgotten about it."

"I'd wager the countess hasn't. And can you imagine her surprise when she learns she is to be the guest of honour?"

"I trust you have no second thoughts about publicly announcing the fact that she is your mother?"

"Only a slight twinge of doubt, but I know I'm doing the right thing. Let's go and find her and introduce her to the seamstresses." He looked at the clock. "I've already written messages to be delivered to the other women of the hat club. It seemed wise to let them know that everything has gone as planned."

"Can you imagine the tales they'll have to tell when word of this gets out?"

"I shudder to think of it. You can bet that no two stories will match."

By the time they found the countess, who had been doing some last-minute embroidery on the shawl she planned to wear to the party, Fredricks had signalled that the seamstresses were being made comfortable in the salon. James explained the situation to the countess and escorted her and Emily downstairs.

They could hear Maria coughing from down the hallway and Emily frowned. "I must ask Cook to prepare a decoction for her. The cherry-bark and lemon were such a help to you when you were ill, Lady Marguerite."

The countess guffawed. "Don't be a ninnyhammer, Emily. I watered the flowers with it. It was the hot rum with a wee sip of brandy that cured me. Never fret. I'll take the woman in hand and she'll be good as new."

James looked at Emily over the top of Marguerite's head and mouthed the words, "God help her."

The butler had no more than opened the door when the room, which had been pleasantly abuzz with the voices of eight excited women, became silent. There was an almost palpable air of expectancy as the trio entered and James bowed to the group.

"Ladies. I would like you to know that thanks to each one of you, our plan has succeeded. It is only a question of time until Grimstead receives the punishment he so richly deserves. My only regret is that you were not here to see him beg for mercy."

Sighs of relief went up around the room. James linked his hands behind his back. "For the present, you are invited to stay in the empty apartments in the servants' hall. Later, we shall see to permanent arrangements. But right now I should like you to meet the rest of my family."

He stepped back and was about to introduce the countess when Polly Bander, who had been staring with undisguised curiosity, stuck her spectacles onto the end of her nose and jumped up.

"Margaret? Margaret McCarthy. Is it you?" She let out a shriek and hobbled towards the countess, her arms outflung. "The saints presarve us. It *is* you. I'd know you anywheres."

The countess took one look at the aging seamstress, clasped her hands to her heart, and fell to the floor in a faint.

Emily grabbed a vinaigrette from the table drawer and passed it quickly under the countess's nose. Polly Bander shrank back against the wall.

"I'm so dreadful sorry. I niver meant to give 'er the vapours, but it surprised me, seein' 'er after all these years."

James motioned the aging seamstress to a chair. "You know her, then? When? Where did you know her?" The urgency in his voice silenced everyone in the room except the countess, who struggled ungracefully to sit up.

"Really, Emily. Must you wave that obscenity in front of my face? Emmett—no, I mean Fredricks! Fetch me a glass of sherry. You, James. Help me to my feet."

James hoisted her into a chair. "Are you all right? Were you hurt?"

"Don't be tiresome, James. I was just a bit giddy." She took a long swig from the glass of sherry and sighed. "Much better. Now tell me just what is going on? I had the strangest thoughts flash before my eyes."

Polly Bander approached more cautiously this time. "I didn't mean to surprise you none, Maggie. You— you are the Margaret McCarthy what used to work for Viscount Addleborough, aren't you?"

The countess looked stunned.

Polly, more than a little uneasy, wrung her hands. "And—and then went on to be the nanny to a boy what belonged to an earl, or some 'igh nob? It must 'ave been nigh on twenty years ago." Her face paled. "I'm awful sorry if I said somethin' I shouldn't 'ave."

Still the countess remained silent. She put her hands to her head and moaned softly. Then slowly the words began to form in her throat as if each syllable were cut and carved individually.

"Margaret. Margaret Elizabeth McCarthy." She rose slowly from the chair and started across the room. Emily and James were close behind her. The countess planted her hands on the wall on either side of the mirror, and stared at her reflection. Unbelieving, she pinched her cheeks and felt her nose, then pulled a grey curl from beneath her mob-cap.

Her voice was strained, as if it belonged to another person. "Upon my word. Can it really be me? Am I Margaret? Margaret McCarthy? Merciful heavens. I believe I am. And all this time I thought I was Marguerite, Countess of Berrington."

The effort was too much for her. She fell to the floor in a dead faint and this time it took several minutes to revive her. James ordered his servants to assist her to her rooms and he and Emily followed them.

The countess looked remarkably small and defenceless when James helped her into a chair near her bed. The fire which had burned so brightly in her eyes seemed to have been extinguished by the revelation of her true identity. James pulled up a chair and sat down in front of her. She stared at the wall, her eyes glazed and unfocused.

Emily, sensing that she should leave them alone, squeezed James's shoulder and started to leave, but he grasped her wrist. "No, Emily. This is for you, too."

She went to stand behind his chair and prayed silently that he would say and do the right thing. She needn't have worried.

He leaned forward, elbows on his knees, and took Margaret's hands in his own. They sat for a moment without speaking. Two large tears spilled from Margaret's eyes and slowly slid down her cheeks. When she made no move to brush them away, James took out a handkerchief and blotted each one in turn.

His voice was thick with emotion. "It's all right, Margaret. I understand."

She turned her head towards him as if the movement brought pain. "James. I didn't know. You must believe that. But even if you do, how can you ever forgive me?"

"I do believe you. And there is nothing to forgive, Margaret."

Her chin quivered. "It should have been your mother who survived. She had so much to live for, and I had nothing. Nothing." She closed her eyes for a moment. "I'll never forget that dreadful night. We were ordered to abandon ship but the lifeboat capsized . . . pulled under as the ship went down. Your mother was struck by a broken spar."

James saw the horror in Margaret's eyes when she opened them, and he touched her hand. "Don't force yourself to remember it tonight, Margaret. We shall have plenty of time to sort things out."

But she continued as if she hadn't heard him. James looked up at Emily and she shook her head.

Margaret spoke quickly as if compelled to lift the burden from her heart. "The waves were so high, and fire—dear heaven, there was fire all about us. Another woman and I tried to lift your mother onto a floating mast but she . . . she must have got tangled in the rigging when she went under and . . . and we never saw her again." Her voice had dropped to a bare whisper.

"Then darkness came as the fire died and I was all alone, clinging to a bit of timber and drifting with the current." She leaned her head back against the chair and closed her eyes.

"Let me call your abigail, Margaret. You need to rest."

"Yes. I'm tired. So dreadfully tired. This is such a blow to me. I've lost everything." Margaret passed her hand over her eyes as if to shut out the memories of that terrible night. Then she seemed to catch a second breath. She leaned forward, grasping his hands intently. "There is something you must know, James."

"Perhaps you should wait."

"No. I must tell you now. I . . . I always dreamed of being a countess. I'll not deny that." She blinked rapidly. "There was a time when you were a boy that I thought of you as the son I'd always longed for. For these past few weeks I believed you really *were* my son. But now I know it was all a hopeless dream. It's *that* loss for which I mourn, James, and not the loss of the title and all that goes with it."

He bent forward and kissed her cheek. "Then you have no need for tears, Margaret, because a kindly fate has brought you back to us. We need you now more than ever. You'll always be a cherished member of my family. I promise you that."

They embraced and Emily had to turn away to hide her own tears.

LATER, after they saw Margaret safely tucked into bed for the night, Emily and James returned downstairs to question Polly Bander. They learned that Polly had been an upstairs maid at the Addleborough country house at the same time that Margaret was nanny to the viscount's four children. The two women had become close friends. It was Margaret who arranged for Polly to live with a family in Kent until she gave birth to her baby girl.

Margaret, who had fallen out of favour with the Addleborough family because of her support of Polly, left their employ and went to work for a family with homes in Brighton and Mayfair. After a few years her charge, a boy, was sent off to boarding school and Margaret was unemployed until she was hired back by the family, a few months later, to act as companion to the countess on an extended ocean voyage. That was the last Polly had heard of Margaret in more than sixteen years.

Both Emily and James pieced the story together and came to the same conclusion. After the shipwreck, Margaret had somehow become confused and, probably without intending to do so, had taken on the identity of Marguerite, the true countess.

James leaned back on the settee as he and Emily sat alone that night in the library sipping chocolate and nibbling on buttered scones. "It's nearly unbelievable but it must have happened that way. And odd though it may seem, I believe every word she told us."

Emily watched the embers glow red, then turn to grey ash in the grate. "It explains why she knew so much about you and your parents and the house."

"I had all but forgotten about Margaret until now. But little things are coming back to me." He broke a scone into pieces and let the crumbs fall at random onto the plate. "They looked very much alike, you know, Margaret and my mother. Even their names were similar.

"I remember how Margaret loved to play games. She'd pretend to be the queen and would send me on all sorts of missions of state. It was her way of teaching me to read, and to follow instructions. But, oh, how she loved to dress up and act the part. I suppose she still does," he mused, "but this time she forgot which one was real and which was the role she was playing."

"What now, James? The party is tomorrow. You can hardly proclaim her as the countess now that we know the truth."

"Neither can I cast her out. She has become like one of the family to me. The truth is that as a child I spent more time with Margaret than with my own mother. I once cared very deeply for her and I find those feelings have returned." He traced the flowered pattern in the silk cover of the settee with the tip of his finger. "The only acceptable solution appears to be to ask her to remain here as a permanent guest and companion. How does that appeal to you?"

"I think it's perfect. She has a good heart. After all, if it were not for Margaret, I would still be running away from Cyrus Grimstead."

"And I would still be bored with life, hoping in vain for a new adventure."

"A game. That's what you said it was. But it's over, James." She leaned towards him and smiled mischievously. "Now you must cast about for something new to occupy your time." She drew her finger down his nose and over his chin. "Whatever will it be?"

He tugged gently at the ringlets clustered at the nape of her neck. "Trust me when I say, Emily my love, that I shall find something close at hand."

EPILOGUE

THE FOLLOWING EVENING the mansion rang with festivity. No one except Emily and James and his solicitor knew that the original purpose of the ball had been to welcome Marguerite as the true countess. When James announced that the party was in honour of his betrothal to Emily, everyone, with the possible exception of a few hopeful debutantes and their doting mothers, celebrated along with them.

Emily and James kept a protective watch over Margaret. They decided that there was nothing to be gained by revealing her true identity, nor would they pretend that she was the genuine Countess of Berrington. Everyone continued to address her as Lady Marguerite, even those few who were aware of her humble background. Most of the ton regarded her as a complete enigma, albeit a delightful one, and that was what she remained.

At least to most people, for there was one exception. A certain Mr. Harrington, a wealthy barrister turned merchant exporter who had previously fallen under her spell, began courting her with unexpected zeal. Margaret blossomed under his attention, but she felt compelled to tell him the truth about her past. Rather than being put off by her lack of a title, he was delighted because it removed what he considered to be the only obstacle standing in the way of their marriage.

Margaret survived her fall from nobility to companion with her usual good humour and strength of character. If James and Emily assumed she would become humble and easily manipulated, they were mistaken, for it was she who was the expert manipulator. It was, in fact, her indomitable spirit which endeared her to them.

Emily and James were married after a short betrothal, and a year later Emily gave birth to a boy, the first of three children. During the Season they lived in the house in Mayfair, but they were most content at the country house near Brighton. Emily continued to meet with the hat club, but they soon adopted the latest craze for creating artistic pictures out of dried flowers or feathers. With the birth of her children, Emily undertook some charitable work for the London Orphanage and found it more satisfying than her artistic pursuits.

In the days which followed the party at Berrington House, Cyrus Grimstead, having gambled away his remaining assets, fled London under cover of darkness. The seamstresses returned to the refurbished rooms over the dress shop and began work on the few orders which remained to be filled. With increasing numbers of debtors to be paid, the constable ordered the shop to be put up for sale.

On a sudden whim, generated no doubt by a pointed suggestion from Margaret, Mr. Harrington bought up the markers, paid the back wages due to the seamstresses, and took over the shop.

Margaret was given free rein to create an entire line of stylish new designs. Orders for gowns and other fripperies began coming in faster than anyone could have hoped, thanks to the ladies of the hat club, who had decided that one attempt at creating their own gowns was quite enough. It soon became known that

Harrington's was the best place in London to find superbly styled and crafted ball gowns. Margaret and her new husband celebrated their success with marriage and a trip to China to buy silks and tapestries for their store.

The eight seamstresses remained at their work, and all were given a share of the business, which would eventually enable them to become self-sufficient. Maria, under the careful supervision of the countess, regained her health and married a well-to-do linen draper. Charity, the youngest of the seamstresses, became mistress to a gentleman of high station and eventually bore his son. The boy was named heir at the age of fourteen to a considerable fortune, a fact which dramatically changed his life and that of his mother.

Countess Lieven became Princess Lieven and continued, in her irrepressible fashion, to manipulate everyone with whom she came in contact. And Yvette? Yvette delighted the Empire with her exquisite voice and her beauty which blossomed further with each new conquest. She was the toast of London Society for nearly a year until a rejected suitor uncovered her secret past. But that, suffice it to say, is yet another story.